ॐ *The Shadow Fighter* ॑

Fiction Series
The Alex Evercrest Series
The River Front
The Girl on The Grill
Missing
Maggot
Racist
Votive Candles
Windy City
Country Road
Pool of Blood
Sins of the Daughter
Body Parts
The Skull Collector
The Vanishing
The Shadow Fighter
Moonshine
Grief's Trajectory
The Magic Touch
Northern Lights
Alex Evercrest Heroine
Alex Evercrest Collection Two
New Direction
Disruption
A Family Affair
The St. Lebuinnus Church Murder

A Brian O'Neil Novel
Hawaiian Phoenix
Moon Curser
Death Broker

The Problem Solver Series
Solutions
Drug Lords
Border Crosser
The Problem Solver Collection

The Taelo Series
Taelo: The Early Years
Taelo: The Golden Feather
Taelo: Journey of Discovery
Taelo: Dangerous Passage
Taelo: Condor Clan Slingers
Taelo: Circumvention
Taelo: The Journey of Sages
Taelo: Collection
Taelo: Future Leaders Journey

A Taelo Story:
White Swan and Quiet Pheasant
The Child's Name
Floating Cloud
Quiet Rabbit
Busy Bee
Little Otter & Talking Wren
Broken Spear
Burley Bear & Meadow Flower
Taelo Story Collection

<u>Science Fiction</u>
The Savitar Series:
Journey's End
Savitar
Confluence
Savitar Series Collection

The Door Series
The Door
Aliens We
The Endless Hole
The Swarm
Esoteric Journey
The Gentle Eye
The Door Series Collection

Bram Nielson Series
The Fold
The Message
Fold Wormhole
Negative Fold
Ripples in Time
Bram Nielson Collection

<u>Single Science Fiction Books:</u>
Current Past and Future
The Event
The Door
Viajante 7

℘ *The Shadow Fighter* ℘

By: *Ron Mueller*

Around the World Publishing LLC
Cincinnati, Ohio

ISBN 13: 978-1-68223-973-5

Distributed by Ingram
Cover Picture by: Pi03@ShutterStock
Cover Design by: Ron Mueller

The Shadow Fighter

1 Enforcer

*A*driano had researched his new home and learned that Chicago was the third largest city in the US. He was taken by its impressive architecture, and vibrant music history. He experienced firsthand why it was known as the Windy City. He walked the entire waterfront and had a faceoff with Lake Michigan and its cold wind coming directly at him.

He knew that it was equally famous for the Mafia families involved in the distribution of booze and drugs. Mafia families that had often been decimated by the violent battles that transpired. The most famous was the St. Valentines Day massacre.

Gennaro Visentino, his predecessor and his mafia leadership team met their demise in a similar way as the 1929 St. Valentine's Day massacre.

He was sent from Itali to take control of what remained of the Mafia organization.

He had moved the Mafia headquarters to another location farther south but still along the shore of Lake Michigan. The location he selected reminded him of the view along Marsala's Contra da Spagnola and his favorite fishing spot on the Sicilian coast where he had fished in his younger days.

He liked to walk along the lake shore and feel the cool breeze as it blew through his dark black hair, and he had found a place where he could cast his line and catch fish.

He recalled and preferred the warmer air, the seaweed, and fish odor of the waters of the salty Tyrrhenian Sea and the fish he caught there. He had only been in Chicago for a few months and was still trying to get use to a much faster and hectic pace of living. His days back in Italy now seemed a luxury as compared to navigating the Chicago competitive drug market. He was taking an aggressive approach and soon hoped to have his organization back to its previous level of drug distribution.

He had reached back to his many loyal Sicilian associates and brought them to Chicago. In a way the ill-fated demise of his predecessor and his entire leadership team had opened the organization at the higher levels, and he was able to establish his loyal followers into those top ranks. This at least provided him a buffer from the struggle the organization faced out in the intense and competitive drug distribution level.

He had moved carefully and slowly to reestablish the Chicago family. It had now been two years since that massacre that was blamed on a black female detective out of Cincinnati.

It was hard for him to envision a single person having been able to eliminate the entire Chicago family.

He personally believed that the main Mexican drug cartel that competed with his organization had a hand in the massacre, but he did not desire to start a war with them, so he was careful as he pushed against them while he slowly regained control of the protection and drug distribution market that the family had previously controlled.

The involvement of a lowly Cincinnati detective was a matter that personally irritated him, and he felt the need to take some sort of retribution action. He sent one of his trusted men to spend time in Cincinnati to observe and get information on this detective.

For six months the reports coming to him indicated that she was careful, was always active in the community and did not seem to be worried about her exposure. She seemed to be just a normal detective that had been very successful.

As he reviewed the information about the cases that she had resolved he came to believe that she was more lucky than smart. He pondered what he should do. His low opinion of her led him to hire and send a sniper to eliminate her. He would have liked to bring her to Chicago to have her go swimming face down in one of the rivers in the city.

He reached back to Sicily to recruit Lorenzo who was considered one of the best assassins in the business. This was a person that he felt would quickly deal with the assassination in and in and out manner.

When Lorenzo arrived, he greeted him, and they agreed on the price. After arranging for him to be provided with a snipers rifle of the design that Lorenzo requested, they agreed that once the assignment was over, a return flight to Sicily out of Cleveland would be paid for.

He knew that it would only be a matter of time until he would get a success report from Lorenzo which then would be followed by a news report on the sad loss of a such a beloved detective in Cincinnati. Not sad for him. He would go out and celebrate the removal of a nuisance.

Alex, that nuisance, had no idea that she had once again become the focus of someone that she had no idea that in some way felt compelled to punish her.

She was busy planning an upcoming fund-raising event with Annie, who she had rescued from fifteen years of chained captivity in the Pennsylvania forest. She was very happy that Annie had made what seemed to be a full recovery from that trauma and now with her two daughters had moved to Maui to live with the person that Annie had met, fallen in love with and whom she called her soulmate.

When Alex received all the paintings that was to be displayed at the Art exhibit, she realized that Annie was now painting prolifically, and her painting reflected a radiance that some of her earlier paintings lacked.

Together they were planning a fund-raising event that was scheduled for mid-July.

She was fund raising for her Helping Hands charity and her Helping Hands retreat.

Annie was holding an art exhibit with Scapes as the theme with forty percent of the sales promised to Helping Hands.

They planned an event at the Cincinnati water front that would feature a band or orchestra that Annie's two daughters, Linda and Lorie were setting up.

She and Matt were celebrating having moved into their new home that they had purchased at an extremely low price. A price that together they had been able to pay off in less than a year. It was the house in Mt Adams where the "Skull Collector" had made the third floor into a skull museum. Alex was converting the museum into one of Art and Rewards. The Art would be many of Annie's paintings, but she planned to also feature paintings of area artists. The featured accomplishments of the young ladies that had gone on from her Helping Hands retreat to make significant improvements in their lives was the other feature of the museum.

She planned to give the first award out as part of the River Front fund raising event.

Back in Maui, Annie, sitting out by the pool was able to see Kekoa and Brian busily discussing their current upcoming trial of Remi Frensby who they had captured out on the Gulf of Mexico. They had been able to influence the trial to begin in the middle of July. This had allowed her and Alex to set their exhibition and fund-raising event at that time.

She was focused on finishing one more painting before focusing solely on the upcoming exhibition in Cincinnati.

Alex was in a great state of mind. She and her detective partners had been enjoying a lull in their usual very busy days.

The Chief was also enjoying the fact that the lull allowed him to give his top two detective teams a rest. He had no idea that the lull was about to end.

Lorenzo flew in from Chicago and registered in one of the top downtown hotels. He was impressed with the downtown area. He spent the next few days checking out the water front. He walked by the area that was being set up for the upcoming art exhibition and concert. He made it a point of going by it several times so he could get the lay of the land.

He located the building that would best serve his needs. It had the right elevation and the right angle that should give him an excellent shot. He was able to get access to the roof to check it out. He hid his sniper's rifle case under an old pallet. All that was left was the wait, the kill shot and then the getaway.

He then took another walk around the area to locate the best place to park his getaway car and to examine the event tents that were in their final stage of preparation. He was impressed with the size of the display tent. It made it clear to him that it was to be a significant event.

He had planned his escape so that it would not involve flying. He figured that he needed to make his way out in a low-key way. He planned on driving out in a used car. Buying a used car was the next thing he needed to do. Once he had the vehicle, he would return to the waterfront park and drive the escape route. He did not want to leave anything to chance. He always worked from a well thought out and choreographed plan.

Alex watched Brenda, Annie's Cincinnati art store partner, as she supervised moving the paintings from the third-floor museum to the air-conditioned tent down at the river front.

Alex had enjoyed housing the art because not only did it erase the memory of the museum with its forty-some human skulls, but it allowed her to have Trey and his family, and the rest of the team enjoy walking through the museum at their leisure.

She had held a house warming party where they had walked through the museum and had each selected the painting they desired. They had all declined the forty per cent discount in favor of having the discount go to her charity.

She had shared that fact with Annie who said that she would bring a special surprise for each of those who purchased a picture early and gave the forty percent to the charity.

Alex let her know that her DEA friend in Chicago and the Head of the IRS in Washington had both purchased a painting.

Alex watched as the last picture was boxed and then carried the three flights to the front door and then the additional steps down to the street. She and Brenda followed the truck down to the River Front parking lot. Once there Alex spent her time focused on looking over the area and ensuring that the refreshment stand that was being set up would have the mix of refreshments she had ordered.

She then went back to the exhibit tent and stepped in from a hot muggy July day into the cool air-conditioning where Brenda was making sure that the art pedestals were stable and that the temperature and humidity was controlled as she desired.

The event was to begin that afternoon and would run over the weekend.

Annie, Brian, Linda, Lorrie, Kekoa, Anela and Brian's parents had all arrived at Lunken airport on Brian's private jet. They all proceeded to check in to the hotel before walking over to the park.

Annie had the special paintings that she had brought as gifts carefully loaded into the private limo that had driven out to the plane. She was eager to see the display that she knew was being set up.

Ten paintings had already been sold, and the show had yet to officially begin. She knew that her parents planned to buy at least one. She went down the list of friends that had said they wanted to buy one of her paintings and she counted at least another ten.

This made her smile as she realized the number of friends she had counted. These were people that had befriended her since Alex had rescued her from the woods of Pennsylvania.

Lorenzo walked into the hotel, and he would have been surprised had he known the artist that was to be featured because he got on the elevator with that person with folks that he figured knew each other well as he went to his fourth-floor room. He felt prepared and was planning to stay in for the rest of the day and then be on the roof early the next morning. He would move his car to be in as close proximity to the parking exit as possible so that once he got his shot off, he would immediately be on his way out of the city.

Alex was just coming out of the art display area to the front packaging and cashier area when she saw Annie and all the rest approaching with a series of boxed cartons that she was sure contained additional paintings.

She and Annie exchanged hugs, and she then hugged everyone else. This was the first time she had met Kekoa and Anela.

She had heard about the escapades that Brian and Kekoa had experienced and was aware that they were to be in court for at least the coming week to attend the trial of the wayward billionaire that they had been responsible for having captured.

She had spent a lot of time coaching Brian and was aware that he had duplicated her feat of shooting out the target's bullseye while being blind folded. She was also impressed with his astounding success at becoming super rich before he turned forty.

Brian was not sure what Annie's and Alex's fund-raising goals might be but he and Kekoa had agreed that they would really put the event in the not to be forgotten category by donating five million dollars.

This they figured was a pittance as compared to more than a billion dollars that the current case they were in Cincinnati to participate in would put into their bank account.

Alex led the way into the art display area. She had the extra pedestals put up for the pictures that Annie had brought as bonuses for every one of her friends.

The pictures were Scapes of the locations that were associated with the locations that each person had close to their homes. She had sent Annie several pictures for the people that Annie knew. These were scapes that she associated with those friends.

For Johnnie she had sent a scape of what Johnnie saw looking out of the bushes of Hyde Park. This was an early scape before Johnnie had become her cyber analyst.

For Mary, Johnnie's significant other, she had a scape of her walking down the street in Philadelphia. That was the day she and Johnnie had first met Mary.

For her parents she had a scape of the lane leading up to the home she had grown up in.

She had the scape of Dexter on his yacht, the Golden Goose, with the barge she had set on fire lighting up the sky behind him.

She had sent in a scape of the capture of a killer in the Mississippi forest that Sheriff Wiggins had led.

She also had the scape of the Chief as he arrived at the scene where she and the team had essentially destroyed the building of a team of gunmen that had made the mistake of trying to resist arrest.

The surprise was when she watched the last painting being placed on a stand. It was her, standing in her bicycle-riding clothes, which made the ripples of her six pack stand out, made her legs look slender and long and her biking shoes still on her feet seemed to be short high heels. She remembered this scene well since she had survived an assassination attempt that took place in front of the public library.

She laughed and said that it was a great painting, but it was not a Scape.

Annie smiled and said that it was an Alex Scape and that if she looked closely at Matt in the background, she would see that he had a great smile on his face.
Alex laughed and gave Annie a hug.

2 The Shots that Should Have

*L*orenzo was up early as he had planned. The stars were still twinkling overhead as he walked across the square to the elevator that would take him down to sub level four. The beads of sweat on his forehead made it clear to him that it was going to be a very warm humid day. He hoped that he would be able to find a shady spot on the roof that he would be lying on.

He moved his car from the basement parking area to street parking near the exit to the River Front Park. He walked along the old rail tracks and then crossed through the pine trees and after checking that no one was around he climbed up on the roof of what he had realized was the park's maintenance building. The sun was just rising, and the day was just beginning to heat up, but he already could feel the humidity climbing. He pulled the bill of his cap down. He hoped that the opportunity for a good shot would be available quickly because as he looked around the roof he was going to be totally exposed to the rising sun.

He stood the old wooden pallet that had been abandoned on the roof on edge so that a shadow was created in the area that he was going to be lying.

He was trying to keep the black surface of the roof as cool as he possibly could. He rolled out his exercise mat that acted like an insulator.

He once again sighted through the scope to make certain he had the position that he wanted. He then lay down to wait. He would have liked to go for a walk, but he did not want to risk being seen climbing up or down from the roof. He accepted the waiting because it was a very common part of his job. He lay down, put his hat over his eyes, and took a nap.

He came awake to the music from a band warming up. He looked over the edge of the roof and saw that people were arriving and staking out their spots on the grassy hill in front of the band stand structure. He saw that many of them had beach umbrellas up. He wished he could have one where he was.

He saw that the concession stand was already doing good business handing out water, soft drinks, coffee, and rolls. He was able to read the menu sign and was impressed that everything was free of charge. He chuckled to himself as he got the urge to go down and get coffee and a roll.

He read the sign in front of the larger tent that invited everyone in for a free showing of *Annie L. Scots*, many Scapes scenes and it added that on exit each person could select a miniature picture of the Scape scene that they liked best.

The second thing that caught his eye was the donation station for an organization called "Young Women's Helping Hands" that offered a second Scape picture for a donation of any amount.

He wondered how any persons associated with the scene below had earned Adriano's ire. It was not something that bothered him, but it did make him wonder because these seemed to be people that he would have wanted to have back in Sicily.

He finally spotted his target as she walked out to look down to where the first band was now playing. He waited until she turned around. He was just pulling very slowly on the trigger when suddenly she was pushed from behind into the tent. He managed to pull his finger off the trigger. He waited for just a second then decided that he had somehow been discovered and decided that it was time to abandon his assassination attempt and make his way to his car slowly but as fast as possible and leave the area. He would try again on another day from another location.

Trey had been following his normal routine when he and Alex were out in public. He was always slightly behind and on one side and at the ready. He was about to ask her if she wanted something to drink when he spotted the laser spot on her back. His reflexes took over and he pushed her as hard as he could into the tent and followed her in. He had expected to get hit but nothing happened.

Alex was surprised at the strength of the push that hurled her through the entrance flap and caused her to stumble and fall just short of hitting the first painting pedestal. She jumped up and reflexively pulled her weapon. Trey put up his hands up.

Alex looked around to see if they had scared anyone and she put her weapon away. He told her about the laser beam. They both cautiously lifted the entrance flap and walked out along the side that was covered. There was only one close by building. They decided to check it out. Both of them would have preferred to have their weapons at the ready but that would have scared the people still arriving for the concert.

They circled around back of what they realized was the park maintenance building and cautiously approached the steel ladder going to the roof. Trey pointed at it and indicated that he was going up and that she should take a few steps back to provide him cover. Once he got to the top of the ladder, he cautiously looked over it and then wave her to come up.

Alex went up and they walked over to where a sniper's rifle and ammunition had been abandoned.

Alex called in to the dispatch center and asked that an investigative team come to investigate the scene of an attempted assassination. She gave the location and instructed those coming to the scene to refrain from using sirens or flashing lights.

She and Trey climbed down from the roof and stood by waiting.

Johnnie had been out by the concession stand flying Gunjfor taking pictures of the crowd when he observed Trey pushing Alex into the tent and following her in. He immediately took Gunjfor up and turned it slowly around and caught someone on the roof of the nearest building crawling to the fire escape in the back.

He took Gunjfor swooping in for a close up but had to pull up to avoid the pine trees. From a higher vantage point, he spotted the person that had left the roof get into a car in the parking lot. He flew Gunjfor toward that location. He was able to get the direction that the car was heading and figured that a quick call to central might get a unit to cut him off and apprehend the person trying to get away.

He brought Gunjfor down and then walked to where he had seen Alex and Trey going.

They were just coming down from the roof when he got there.

Alex looked at him and asked if by chance he had been able to get anything with Gunjfor.

Johnnie smiled, shook his head, and said that he had the backside of the shooter and the back side of the getaway car, but he did not have much else but behinds of some person and that person's car. The licensed plate had a grey cover that hid the license plate.

Alex asked to see what Johnnie had captured. As she watched the video, she said that she wanted to get the information to the lab so that the photo analysts could do an in-depth detailed analysis.

She said that the shoes, the shirt, and pants might all hold a clue as to who that person might be. She pointed to the license plate that had a grey cover that seemed make the license plate unreadable but perhaps the analysist might be able to see through it. The rear of the car had no auto make emblems, so she figured the shooter was a professional.

Johnnie got on line and sent the footage to the lab. Then he said that he was going back to filming the event.

Alex thanked Trey for literally having her back and gave him a hug.

Trey nodded and said that it was not often that he got the opportunity to shove her around. He then said that he was ready to enjoy the rest of the day with Nolan and Lesley.

Alex asked where they were.

Trey said that when he shoved her into the tent they were walking and looking at the Scape paintings. He added that Lesley had observed what had happened and had guided Nolan to the back of the tent. He figured he would have to explain the situation to them.

Alex shook her head and commented that she had no idea why she was on someone's hit list.

Trey laughed and replied that she had left a trail of bodies, people in prison and destroyed gunships and burned down coal barges that left a huge number of potential people mad enough that they might think about trying to do her in.

Alex said that she agreed that there was a long trail but that he was exaggerating the number of people left alive to try to get revenge.

Trey agreed and said that no one came to mind.

Alex said that it was similar to the Scape scene Annie had captured of what she called the Alex Scape painting that was featured as the first painting when a person entered the display tent. That was a case where a racist had decided to kill her because her skin color offended him.

Lindsey was standing pointing to the picture of the Scape that featured their backyard. It was of Nolan, Linda, and Laurie on the swing set. This was a painting that she had purchased during Alex's private showing of Annie's Scapes when Alex had hosted a party for all her friends. She was thrilled to be able to get a painting of the time several years ago when the kids were younger. The three kids were now at least six or seven years older and no longer children but young adults.

She saw Alex fly in and sprawl on the floor and immediately jump up with her weapon pulled. She watched as Trey followed her in. Alex immediately put her weapon away and the two of them cautiously left the tent.

She guided Nolan to the back of the tent expecting gunfire but there was none. She continued guiding Nolan around to take in all the different Scapes that Annie had painted.

She was hesitant to leave the tent and engaged Annie in conversation.

Trey returned and saw that Lindsey was still in the tent. He walked over and asked if she was ready to go sit out on the lawn and listen to the music.

She asked what had happened.

Trey responded that nothing had happened and that was a good thing. He said that he would share more once he knew more.

Nolan laughed and said now he understood why he had been kept in the tent. He then added that he was ready for something to drink, something to snack on, and he wanted to listen to the bands that Linda and Lorie had chosen for the event.

Trey took Lindsey's hand and led the way out.

Brian had been in the tent watching Annie as she walked around and engaged the people looking at her paintings. He had observed Alex as she flew in and landed at the base of the first picture. He remained seated but was ready to act if necessary. He called to Kekoa who was out on the lawn with Anela and asked if there was anything strange going on. He listened as Kekoa replied that things were calm, and the only action was on the stage. Kekoa added that the two girls had done a great job in selecting the first opening group.

Brian had noticed Lindsey's reaction, so he walked over and talked to her and Nolan. He knew that Annie considered Lindsey a good friend and the two girls still argued in fun as to who got to marry Nolan.

It seemed like quite a while before Alex and Trey returned but it was clear to him that they had things in control.

He walked over to Annie and asked if he could get her anything.

Lorenzo made his way to the highway and drove north. He was keeping his speed just below the speed limit and staying to the right most lane. He was thinking about what he needed to do. He definitely needed to find a place to stay for the night. It needed to be an out of the way place where he could get something to eat and hopefully buy a different car. He needed to shed all connection with his stay in Cincinnati.

He hoped to circle back and get a second chance at what he had been hired to do.

He drove until a sign loaded with fast food places and another that highlighted a number of hotels caught his eye. He figured that it was time to get something to eat and then get a room for the night and get some sleep.

In the morning after a quick breakfast, he drove around the area and found a used car lot that seemed to have a good offering of cars for sale. He found a car that seemed to be in good shape, and he traded in his current vehicle for the car plus a thousand dollars more.

He knew that the dealer was getting a good deal and if he had been in Italy, he would have bargained for a better deal for himself.

He decided that he would rather get a different car and leave a happy dealer versus one that felt pressured to make the exchange.

He did not want to be remembered.

He called in to Adriano and let him know what had happened. He shared that he was returning to Cincinnati to finish the job, but he needed another sniper's rifle.

Adriano was surprised by the call but pleased that Lorenzo was planning to finish the job. He let Lorenzo know where he could pick up another sniper's rifle. He asked when he should expect the news of the targets demise.

Lorenzo replied that he was going to spend the day deciding on a new location for his next assassination attempt. He wanted a location that gave him a great shot and an easy escape. The location would depend on his targets movement.

He spent the next couple of days observing his target's morning and evening transit to and from work. She had a route down the steep hill from her home to a transit area where she crossed the highway and then rode past an apartment building where she was joined by an older bicycler who then took the lead. The route down to the apartment building was consistent but the route from there to the police station varied randomly on each of his observations.

He decided that the best place for the shot was as she came down the steep hill and crossed on the road over the highway.

He then spent time identifying the best location that would give him a good shot and an easy get away. He decided that the best location was as she got to the bottom of the hill and was getting ready to cross over the US 71 highway.

He found a way to take the service elevator to the roof. There he found a good spot and set everything up.

On Tuesday morning Alex departed from her house and rode slowly down the steep hill that took her to the point where she crossed over US 71 to get into the downtown. She loved where her house was located and the great view it provided but the way to work was a challenge and she was currently replacing her bicycle brake pads once a week because she had to engage them almost continuously to get safely down the hill.

She was crossing the bridge when a careless driver put her so close to the wall that she had to brake and push herself off the wall to keep from going over the side. As she did so the head tube of the bike shattered. As she went over her handle bar she rolled and drew her weapon. She came up behind a car stopped for the red light. She looked up at the buildings on the other side. She saw a glint. She moved immediately to her right and heard the bullet hit the cement behind her. She took three shots. One at the glint and two on either side of the glint. At the range and the upward angle, she was shooting she was not sure she had chosen the correct angle.

The stop light turned green, and she jogged along with the cars as they made the left turn at the light. She then ran across the intersection and to the base of the building. She stopped at the entrance and called in a shot fired, and an officer needing backup and gave the address. The sirens and the flashing lights of the approaching police cars were visible in less than two minutes.

Alex explained the situation and that the shooter had been on the roof, but she was not sure where he might be at the moment.

She watched as the Chief accompanied by Trey and Johnnie got out of his car and came over to her.

She pointed to where her bike was laying at the side by the wall of the road and said that was where she had first encountered being shot at and that there was another point about fifteen feet in front of that where the second bullet hit the wall.

The Chief called one of the police officers and asked him to tape of the area along the bridge that was part of the crime scene but to keep traffic flowing.

He then asked if she was OK.

Alex nodded and replied that she was going to have a few sore spots from having rolled over her handle bar, but her helmet and pads had saved her.

Johnnie had launched Gunjfor and made her fly to the top of the building. He then showed everyone where the shooter happened to be. The picture showed a large hole in the back of a person's head.

Gunjfor had arrived just as a squad of officers came across the roof with their guns drawn. One of them waved to the camera and gave a thumbs up as he pointed to the body lying face down.

Johnnie kept Gunjfor hovering until Dr Rogers arrived and gave his thumbs up while his team took pictures before he turned the dead shooter over.

He then loudly commented that only a person who shot out bull's eyes blindfolded could do the kind of shooting with the kind of results that he was seeing.

Alex said that it was time she got a ride into work and walked towards the Chief's car.

He stopped her and threw his keys to her and said that when the site was totally in control, he would re-turn to the office, and they should discuss the case. He wanted to find out who was behind the current attempts on her life.

3 The Ground Hog's Paradox

*A*lex entered the station's ladies changing area, got out of her bicycle riding clothes, and sat down for a moment. She kept thinking about how similar the latest attempt on her life was to the day she had survived being shot off her bike as she bicycled into work a couple of years ago. It seemed too similar to be targeted in almost the same way. Then she had slowed down to avoid a hole in the street. That slight fraction of time altered the trajectory of the bullet meant for her head and instead it hit her backpack and ruined the computer that it carried. She had shot and killed the person doing the shooting and the person driving the light blue pickup with the gunman in the back. They died; she survived. But survival had been followed by a longer period of finding out the why and who wanted to take that pre-emptive action against her. Pre-emptive action that she later learned was driven by the color of her skin.

That fact had affected her more than she had been prepared for. She was used to obvious discrimination because of the color of her skin but to have someone try to kill her made the study of the time of Martin Luther King mean so much more to her than it had when she was in school.

This time a rude driver had caused her to brake and try not to be thrown over the overpass to the street below. That slight momentary slow down meant her bicycle was hit.

She had to roll over her handle bars in a very similar way as she did on the first occasion and her subsequent actions had allowed her to kill the sniper trying to kill her. Now she was wondering whether it was a pre-emptive or reactive action that the assassination attempt was based on.

After a moment, she walked out to the bull pen area where Bill and Trevor were sitting talking to Trey and Johnnie.

Bill looked at her and asked if she was OK.

Trevor smiled and added that he knew she was OK and went on to ask if she knew who was after her.

Alex shook her head and said that she thought she would name what had happened to her as "the ground hog's paradox" because it felt like she was living a previous experience over again. She felt that some person had decided that she should be killed. It was most likely some person who she did not know but held some grudge against her. She added that she hoped that the why would become clear.

She pointed at Trey and thanked him for saving her the first time on Saturday morning.

She added that she would now like to thank the rude driver of the car that almost pushed her over the guard rail to the street below. That moment had caused the sniper to miss.

The two assassination attempts clearly meant that somebody wanted to kill her and like the time a couple of years ago, she had no idea where to begin with tracking down the person behind the current situation.

Bill asked her to remind him how the team had identified the person responsible for the first shooting.

Alex was quiet for a moment and then shook her head. She commented that it was more or less pure luck. She had spotted a stripe on a car with the same color of paint as that of the pickup used in the shooting. The owner of the car had given her the location of where she had recently bought the car and two amazing detectives, Bill, and Trevor, had identified the shooter.

Trevor laughed and then added that they had all almost met their end except for the fact that Cincinnati's Black Annie Oakley had single handedly repelled the person who ruined a perfectly good fishing outing on lake Michigan.

The Chief walked in and said that he wanted everyone in his office in five and then went into his office. It was clear to the team that he was not in a good mood.

Alex said she was getting a cup of coffee and hoped that there was a bear claw left in the donut box.

Once they were all in the office the Chief looked around and asked if anyone could make any sense out of what had happened on Saturday and again this morning.

Alex said that it was a repeat of what had happened when a racist had decided that her skin color offended him. She felt this case was based on some offense that she was being held accountable for. She added that the two organizations that she had recently offended the most was the Mafia and the Gulf Cartel, but she had no clue if either of those organizations had a current personal vendetta against her or a contract out on her. She added it could just be a repeat of the first time based on the color of her skin.

Bill suggested they contact the "Angel on the hill" and ask her to find out if she had any idea if one of the Mexican cartels was involved.

Johnnie said he would contact her and ask.

Alex thanked Bill for the good idea. She said that instead of contacting her friend on the hill, they instead talk with Adolfo, her brother, who was in town. He and his wife had arrived on the weekend to attend Annie's art showing and to personally donate a large sum of money to her Helping Hands charity. She was having dinner with them in the evening.

She added that if it was not one the cartels then it might be harder to figure out who in the Mafia might be responsible.

The Chief suggested that he talk with the Illinois lieutenant governor and ask her if she had any idea about a mafia connection.

Alex nodded and added that she was sure the mafia might blame her for the fact that the entire Chicago Mafia Leadership team had been killed even though she had been out fishing when it happened.

Matt and his EMT team had arrived at the shooting site with the fire trucks and had taken in the scene. He realized that the bike that was taped off in yellow tape at the side of the over pass was Alex's. He caught sight of Alex still in her riding clothes, catching a set of keys from the Chief and then getting into the Chief's car with Trey and driving away.

He knew that she was OK, so he relaxed and spent time talking to the police lieutenant in charge of the scene. He stayed clear of the Chief because it was obvious, he was steaming mad.

The police lieutenant describe the amazing shots that Alex had taken. All three shots had hit the sniper.

He and his team soon learned that the sniper was being examined by the coroner. He knew that Dr. Rogers would be giving Alex a hard time for over working him and his team. He marveled at the relationship Alex had with him. Alex hated the morgue and Dr. Rogers insisted that his reviews be done in the morgue. He would take his time, and he always had the corpse exposed and made sure to point out all the gruesome wounds. The smell of the morgue added to the discomfort that Alex felt.

She had shared with him that she often insisted that the Dr. come to her meetings as revenge. Matt had laughed and said that the Dr. had the upper hand in that situation since he always ended up with a cup of coffee and a donut when he came to her meetings, whereas she ended up nauseous.

He and the team had nothing to do for a few moments so they agreed to go to the police station so that he could touch base with Alex.

Alex was just leading the team to the huddle room when she saw Matt and his team walking in.

Matt smiled commented that he and his team were too late to save her at the crime scene, so they figured to come down and see if there were any donuts left in the coffee area.

Alex reached up and gave him a hug and said he and his team could have anything in the coffee area, but she and her team were going to go in and figure out how to handle this ground hogs day case.

Matt nodded and said he understood and that he was happy to see her taking the lead to figure out what was going on.

Alex reminded him that they had a dinner appointment with Adolfo and his wife and then turned and headed for the huddle room.

When they sat down Johnnie confessed that he had contacted Adolfo and asked him about any Cartel vendettas against her.

He apologized about doing so but added that he and Adolfo had been exchanging texts since his arrival in Cincinnati because they had become fairly close since the time, they had collaborated on the Votive Candles case.

Alex replied that no apology was needed and asked what Adolfo's response had been.

Johnnie replied that Adolfo said he was ninety-nine percent sure that there was no cartel involvement but that he would check and verify his belief.

Alex nodded and said if that was the case, they needed to figure out the Mafia connection.

The Chief walked in and shared that he had just finished talking with the Illinois Lieutenant Governor who was surprised that her star employee had faced two attempted assassinations. He added that he had let her know that the employee they were talking about was his and not hers.

She volunteered that she had recently been informed of the aggressive nature of the new Chicago mafia boss by the Chicago Chief of Police. It seemed that this boss, Adriano Barbieri, had imported a significant number of folks from Sicily and was challenging the Gulf cartel for more control of the Chicago drug distribution market.

Alex asked if they had talked about her status as a special agent working for Jane being reinstated.

The Chief smiled and said that Jane had offered to reactivate her and Trey's status of working for her on special assignment but that this time the two of them would have to take a promotion and a pay raise.

Alex nodded and said that then she was set and ready to go. She added that she would appreciate Johnnie, Bill and Trevor being available to support her if things mushroomed.

The Chief smiled and said that her support was in place to be used as needed. He then looked at her and asked if her time in Chicago included a fishing trip for her team and smiled and said that he was on her team.

Alex laughed, shook her head, and then looked around and said that as soon as she figured out the timing of her assignment, she would schedule another fishing trip that included everyone in the office and their significant others.

Johnnie said they should all give a Marine "hurrah" for their upcoming fishing trip since he was sure Alex would soon solve the mystery of the ground hog's paradox.

Alex was sure that anyone outside of the office was wondering about the "hurrahs" that shook the walls.

Alex looked at Trey and asked if he was ready to go to Chicago to get a first-hand look at what might be going on.

She looked at Johnnie and asked him to dig into the new Mafia leader's actions, bank accounts and to get any other personal information he could. She wanted to be armed with as much information as possible.

Johnny smiled and said he was having his own ground hog's paradox because this was exactly what she had asked him to do several times before.

Trevor laughed and said that he too was having one, but it was about being left out and lonely, something that always brought tears to his eyes.

Alex smiled and replied that she would brush any tears from his eyes when he got that lonely.

The Chief once again knew that these two teams had a very close working relationship that spoke to Alex's ability to pull them all together.

4 The Windy City

As the early morning flight to Chicago took a swing out over the lake as it made its approach Alex looked down at Lake Michigan's blue waters, pointed out the window that she could see her favorite fishing spot.

Trey leaned over to look out the window and jokingly said he too could see the red x that marked the fishing spot.

Alex looked at him and asked if he knew that Lake Michigan was the only one of the five Great Lakes of North America that was located entirely within the United States.

Trey shook his head and said until she had just told him he had never thought about it.

She went on to say that Lake Michigan had the longest north to south stretch of all the Great Lakes. This gave the region around it a very diverse climate, which allowed and supported the wide variety of plant and animal species in the area. She said the lake boasted a variety of natural habitats, including tall grass prairies, wide savannas, and the world's largest freshwater sand dunes.

The lake had fascinated her all her life and she continued to be amazed at how each time she returned home she learned something new and once again fell in love with the area.

She said that Chicago was home to some of the world's most iconic buildings. She said that this time she wanted to visit the Frank Lloyd Wright Home and Studio. And if they had time, they should also go to the Museum of Contemporary Art including the Sears Tower.

Trey said that he loved the Chicago-style hot dogs and the Chicago-style deep dish pizza and that they would have to take time to enjoy that. The rest of what she had planned would most likely be new to him.

The plane turned and the long coast line north toward Evaston came into view. Alex pointed out and said that she could see the buildings at North Western University where her father taught and where she had gone to school. She smiled and said that it felt good to be coming home but the reason for her return was eating at her.

Alex commented that when she grew up, she was taught that looking at the lake was always to look to the East. If she kept that in mind, she would always be able to navigate the north and south that had built up and flourished at its shore.

The plane was on its final approach as she commented how much she loved Lake Michigan. She shared the fact that her summers would have been incomplete without dips in the lake and fishing with her father.

She added that the winters would have been a lot more manageable were it not for Lake Michigan's unforgiving cold freezing winds.

She and Trey had traveled light and pulled their suit cases along behind them and went out past the security area. She was surprised to see her father standing waiting for them. After giving him a hug she asked why he had come to pick them up.

He laughed and said it was the only way to bring her jag to her so she could enjoy it every moment she was home. He asked to pull her suit case but led the way when Alex refused.

She was happy to be able to drive the car that was her prize possession. She had not taken it to Cincinnati because it seemed that every vehicle or car, she drove there ended up with bullet holes in them or ended up ablaze to become a melted deformed cinder. Since she had started driving the departments oldest car it seemed that no one wanted to shoot at her.

On the drive home she looked over at Trey and asked if he knew that Chicago was founded by a Black trapper, Jean Baptiste Point du Sable Chicago's first permanent settler in 1779, a trapper and merchant credited with building the trading post that evolved into Chicago. She added that he hailed from Haiti and settled into what is now Chicago with his Ptawatomi wife, Kittihawa.

Her father added that Jean was honored in Chicago by having the Jean Baptiste Point DuSable Lake Shore Drive, DuSable Bridge on Michigan Avenue, and the DuSable Museum of African American History all named after him.

He pointed out that he taught this in his philosophy classes, and it always surprises most of his students.

Trey looked back and said that it surprised him because he had never been taught that fact in any of his history classes.

Alex chose to take the surface streets instead of the highway. She preferred to enjoy her drive along the lake and through the universities along the way. It took her back a few years to when she had been going to Northwestern.

The driveway leading to the house seemed to have again grown thicker and the view of the house was like looking through a tunnel. It brought back so many good memories that she felt on the verge of tears.

Some distance south along the Lake Michigan shore line; Adriano was just getting into his office. He walked over to the window as he held his fresh cup of coffee and looked out over the beach area to the calm early morning lake.

He had received that startling news that his assassin had been killed. Apparently, he had been shot by the person he had been sent to assassinate. That seemed impossible and it made him wonder about the capability of the Black female detective.

He had his hands full dealing with the Mexican cartel competition.

He was upset about what he had thought to be an easy elimination of the person that had caused the Mafia to have a huge setback was turning out not to be as easy as he had thought it would be. He hoped to figure out some way to deal with his personal irritation.

He planned to discuss this situation with his inner group of the leadership team to see if they had any ideas.

Rose-Anne came out and gave Alex a long hug and said that she had talked with Jane about the reason for the trip and was about to apologize for her involvement in the original Mafia situation but stopped when Alex put her finger on her lips. She remembered Alex's instruction not to apologize unless she was the instigator.

She instead turned and gave Trevor a hug and said they should all go into the house. She added that she had nothing planned for lunch, but she was planning to cook a rib steak for each of them for dinner.

Alex said that a late dinner would be good because she planned to take two bikes with her down to Chicago's lakeshore bike path and bike into the downtown area, around the downtown and perhaps take in a museum or two as part of her surveillance of the situation.

Her father said he would get the bike rack mounted and the bikes ready for action and went out to the garage.

Alex thanked him and said that they would get lunch along the way because Trey wanted to enjoy either a Chicago hot dog or a Chicago deep dish pizza.

Trey said that sounded great as long as she did not plan to ride the entire eighteen miles of the bike path that ran along the shore.

Alex replied that she was planning to ride the Lakefront Trail closer to the downtown that connected to many of Chicago's most popular parks and beaches. This would facilitate doing the ride in just several hours versus in days.

She said that she had heard from a friend that the GLS café that was alongside the Lakefront bike trail was great and had a simple but good menu.

Trey said that as soon as he put his suitcase in his room and changed into his cycling outfit, he would be ready to go.

Alex said that she would be ready to go in about ten minutes.

Adriano was at the same time discussing with his leadership team what should be done about what had happened in Cincinnati. He was personally fuming about the situation.

Almost unanimously his team said that he should just drop the issue and focus on Chicago because they had their hands full with multiple small gangs that kept fighting with each other but also the fight for control of the drug market that needed their attention. They pointed out that they had had strong competition on a more dangerous level with the Gulf cartel, who were well organized and well-armed.

Adriano thanked them for their honest and direct view point and said he would consider their advice.

On the drive to the parking spot she had in mind, Alex shared the fact that Chicago's motto "urbs in horto" or city in a garden adopted in the 1830's alluded to the city's large, impressive, and historic park system. She planned to see much of it on the ride.

She said that of special interest to her favorite partner was the fact that in 1943, Ike Sewell invented Chicago deep dish pizza at his restaurant Pizzeria Uno, where it was still served to this day.

She added that they would bicycle through the area known as the Loop that followed the elevated "L" train tracks. She said that she felt that this area would give them a firsthand look at the drug traffic. She had no idea who controlled the drugs in this area but in her mind, it would provide a street level look at what was going on.

As they rode their bikes along the loop, she pointed out Jeanne Gang's Vista Tower that at the time it was built was the world tallest structure to be designed by a woman. She had graduated from the University of Illinois in Champaign-Urbana and later became a professor at the Harvard School of architecture. Alex added that she had found out that Jeanne's award-winning work had redefined Chicago's skyline.

Other of Jeanne's work in Chicago included the Nature Boardwalk at Lincoln Park Zoo and two boathouses along the Chicago River.

The bike ride would take them close to the DuSable Museum of African American History where she planned to stop for a quick walk through.

Trey said that it sounded great to him but he wanted to make sure that the restaurant stop was one of the first so he could recover from having to keep up with her but also, he figured that by then both of them would need to take a break.

The ride along the "L" seemed to be a series of staged drug exchanges that were clearly obvious and seemed to be happening at about every other alley way as they rode the loop.

They then headed toward the DuSable Museum of African American History and continued to see the proliferation of the drug distribution.

Once they were in the museum Alex focused on enjoying what was being shared. She had purchased a personal tour that provided a tour guide.

She learned about:

The Chicago resident Gwendolyn Brooks who became the first African American woman to win a Pulitzer Prize in 1950 for her book Annie Allen.

Senator Carol Moseley Braun, the country's first female African American U.S. senator who was elected in 1992.

She learned that though born in New York, Michael Jordan became synonymous with Chicago as he lead the Chicago Bulls to six National Basketball Association championships and earning the NBA's Most Valuable Player Award six times.

Clarinetist, composer, and band leader Benny Goodman, aka "The King of Swing," was born in Chicago.

Legendary contemporary jazz pianist, composer, and on-air jazz host Ramsey Lewis was currently a Chicago native.

And she was remined that Barack Obama, was a Chicagoan who was elected the 44th President of the United States to become the first African American to serve in the office.

She felt the trip to the museum had been well worth her time and the tour had lasted twice as long as she had planned because she had lost track of the time as she listened to her tour guide.

She thanked her for the tour and gave her a generous tip.

Trey commented that almost everything that they had seen and talked about was new to him and he wanted to bring Lindsey and Nolan to take a tour of the museum.

Alex was pleased with Trey's reaction because she had been a little apprehensive about what his reaction might be.

Just a few blocks away Adriano had just received a call from his Cincinnati informant that Alex Evercrest had taken a flight to Chicago. He was immediately concerned about that situation and wondered if she had somehow figured out that the mafia was connected to the assassination attempts.

He decided to tap into his Chicago network to see if he could find out where she might be staying.

Had he known that he, his home life, his bank accounts, and his criminal actions were all being analyzed he would have been even more worried.

5 Discovery

*A*s they rode their bikes back to where the car was parked Alex looked to the west and took in the Chicago skyline that was a black silhouette against the yellow-red tinged rays of the setting sun. A strong breeze from the right was delivering a cooling chill that provided imputes to quickly get to the car.

Trey commented that the lake seemed determined to blow him off the trail and that he was ready to get back to the house and enjoy a cup of hot tea.

Johnnie had spent the day hacking his way through a variety of firewalls as he pursued information on Adriano. He was surprised at the ease with which he got through the Mafia firewall. The information that he was able to extract was a great road map of the drug distribution network that was operated in Chicago. He was sure that Alex would be able to work with Harold Zimmerman, the DEA leader, to make a significant impact in reducing the drug flow in Chicago. He knew that Alex and Harold had close relationship that went back several years.

He had traced Adriano's Mafia history back to Sicily and had learned of his disciplined and rather hard-edged rise up the mafia hierarchy. Johnnie recognized that he approached his assignments with a thoroughness and intensity that left his competitors standing at the sidelines. It was clear that he had caught the eye of the mafia heads.

When the Chicago mafia organization was wiped out, Adriano was the one that was identified to reestablish the Chicago branch. Johnnie found an e mail that stated the expectation that he was to expand the Chicago market and to negotiate with the Mexican cartels to supply the drugs but to remove the Cartel organization presence from Chicago. He figured that this last expectation would be extremely hard to negotiate and might very well lead to a gangland war.

He then tracked the way the money was managed. He traced the money that was brought in by the street drug distributors and stayed locally. He traced the money that was paid to various organizations for various drugs, and he traced the money that made its way to the offshore accounts.

Johnnie was surprised at how many different groups produced a variety of drugs locally. Many of the names of these drugs were totally new to him and he had to do some research to learn what effect each had. He was surprised that anyone would ingest such devastating and harmful substances that produced some sort of short term high, or hallucination followed by a long-term negative impact on almost every organ in the body.

His conclusion from what he was able to learn was that the drug business was very lucrative and that its customers were willing to pay whatever price was set at. The only thing that kept the situation under control was the competition between various distributors of the drugs.

Johnnie concluded that illicit drug making, and distribution was very similar to the legal drug making and distribution system.

He organized all that information and sent it to the rest of the team.

Alex was glad to be back at her Jag. After getting their bicycles secured in the bike rack, she got in and put up the top. Without the lake wind, the car was comfortable and actually felt warm. On the drive back to the house, Trey told her of the information that Johnnie had gathered about the current Mafia leader and his organization.

The thing that stood out to Alex was that Adriano, as she now thought of him, was a person that liked everything to comply with his will and that those who did not meet his wish were either pushed aside or eliminated. She felt that he was the type of person who would send an assassin to Cincinnati to eliminate a person that he felt had done something detrimental to the Mafia organization.

She was at a loss how she was going to prove such a connection and if she established the connection how she would handle that situation. It seemed to her the story of the chicken and the egg; which came first?

Adriano was incensed by the failure of his assassin and agitated further by the fact that the person responsible for killing him was in the Chicago area. He was pushed farther along his line of anger by the fact that his leadership team had suggested they not deal with this single individual whose jurisdiction was in Ohio. They had suggested that they all focus on the Chicago distribution area. He felt ignored and he did not like the feeling.

He had listened to their view point but was not inclined to follow the advice they were giving him.

He instead called in two of his field enforcers and gave them the order to go to the address in Evanston and eliminate everyone that resided there. The elimination order stressed that it was to happen that evening around the normal dinner time. They were to go in kill everyone that was in the house. They were to take a picture of each individual so that he had proof that the black detective was indeed among the dead.

After they left his office, he spent a few moments thinking through the time it would take. He then left for a walk along the beach before going home. As he walked slowly kicking at a broken stick that had washed up on the beach, he wondered what the local police in Evanston would do about the carnage they would walk into when they were called to the scene.

Since the killings would be done in the house, he hoped there would be a multiple day delay before they were discovered.

He would have loved to be there to witness the carnage. He turned and walked back to where his black limo and driver were waiting to take him home.

Ray and Baily were both friends from their days in the growing up on Chicago's south side. They had been basketball stars in high school and then they worked together in a fast-food kitchen cooking fry's, burgers and making chili. Every day after work they looked for a pickup basketball game. It was during one of the games that they were approached about getting into distributing drugs. When they found out how much money they could make it was a no-brainer. They jumped at the chance and went enthusiastically giving what they were doing no second thoughts.

Then one day they were pounced on by four members of an opposition gang. It took them more than a month to recover from the beating and they each had scars from stab wounds and Ray had a long scar across one cheek.

They decided that they would get even. After buying two, three fifty sevens and several hundred rounds of ammunition from the back of a grey van, they went out on the hunt for their attackers. Their approach was to find one of the attackers and without any warning shoot that person in the head. Their revenge was swift with no fanfare and kept as low key as possible. Low key meant that the police had no clue what was going on.

Their drug supplier must have known because he asked them if they wanted to move up to being enforcers.

They jumped at the opportunity when they found out what an enforcer could make for occasionally doing more than threatening a store owner or whacking some person about to remind them not to cheat on the protection money they were to cough up.

Their actions and effective way of running the protection business soon got them promoted to reporting directly to the Mafia leadership team. This meant a different more violent level of enforcement. They both realized that they like what they were doing.

They had been out doing their job when the entire Mafia leadership team had been wiped out.

Adriano had kept them as his enforcers when he came to Chicago to take the Mafia reigns.

He had personally called them into his office. They both were overcome as they stood and listened to what he wanted them to do. He made it clear that they would receive a significant bonus for a successful hit job. He asked them if they were ready for this next step up on the enforcer scale. They had both answered that they were ready to do whatever they were asked to do.

The up-front sum of money promised blew their minds. The amount promised for a successful job was three times as much.

They looked at each other and smiled. They both knew they were going to be rich.

They were surprised to be given an address and told to go into the home and kill everyone. They were to leave no finger prints, no bullet casings, no evidence that could be used to trace the killings. It was to be an in and an immediate out job. They were to use the car that was waiting for them in the parking garage and when the they were done the car was to be returned and they were to leave the building, walked at least six blocks into the city and take a cab home to where they lived.

They stopped at the basement armory where there was a huge array of untraceable weapons to select the weapons, they felt would be most effective for the job. They were in awe of the variety that they could choose from.

They were really impressed with the bore of the four-gauge shotgun. They could put their finger into the barrel. When they saw the size of the brass shells and the shiny slug casings, they immediately picked it. They figured they would be unstoppable with such weapons in their hands.

They were now driving to a location where they would be stepping into the really big league of carrying out their role. They joked about how they would be able to walk in and blow anyone that was there in two with the weapons they had picked. They were both impressed as they drove through what seemed to be a tunnel with a huge home at the other end.

They parked and walked up to the door and Bailey stepped up and kicked the door expecting it to buckle and cave in. Instead, he almost fell down and hurt himself. His leg ached from the kick he had delivered.

Ray pulled him back and fired his shotgun. They both expected the door to explode and shatter as they stepped forward. They both ran into a solid closed door.

Alex was sitting with everyone else out by the pool as they were just finishing dinner when the racket at the front door occurred.

Her father laughed and said that whoever was trying to break in had just tested the door he had made.

Alex signaled Trey to follow her, and she rushed through the kitchen to the garage and went to the door that opened out toward the front door of the house.

She quietly said that she would take the kneeling position and that Trey should take the high position.

She then opened the door and yelled out to the two men standing at the front door to throw down their weapons and surrender. She was just about to say they were under arrest when both men turned toward her. She saw the weapons they had in their hands and fired two shots. Both shot guns went off and blew out a huge section of the front flower bed.

Trey had simultaneously fired his weapon.

Ray heard a female telling him to throw down his weapon and figured he would blow her away. He was turning to do so when the world went black.

Alex rushed out ready to fire again but realized that between her and Trey each of the two gunmen were twice dead.

She looked around to see if there was anyone else involved and rushed out to the car to verify that there was no one there. She also noted that there did not seem to be any law enforcement on the way in.

She called 911 to report a shooting and gave the address. She then went to the front door and rang the doorbell. Her father peeked through the crack as he opened the door.

He opened the door and pointed to the flattened slug that was imbedded in the wood. He then pointed to the hinge area where the edge of a half inch steel plate was visible.

Alex asked when he had the door installed.

Her father laughed and said that he had decided to build a special door after her last visit when she had sent a burning coal barge to the bottom of Lake Michigan. He had figured that with a daughter that took on drug pushers, drug cartels and the Mafia he needed to do something to keep his home safe.

Alex gave him a hug and thanked him for being proactive. She then asked that he go back to the pool area and assure his significant other that everything was in control.

She went out to where the car was parked, put her weapon on the hood and asked Trey to do the same. She then walked over to the flower bed situated between the front door and the garage and sat down. She wondered where the slug that had plowed through the flower bed and up rooted the three rose bushes would be found.

She would see that the rose bushes were put back into their original locations.

She watched as three police cars came up the lane toward them.

She was already thinking what her response should be for an obvious Mafia hit job.

She quietly asked Trey who he thought would be able to activate such a response to their presence in Chicago.

Trey had been thinking about the same thing. He was certain that only the top Mafia leader could possibly have the resources and the means to put a hit so quickly into motion.

Alex then said that she thought that it was the Mafia leader himself and that she wanted to immediately act to hit back. She said that she was going to see if Harold and the DEA would take immediate action. She said that she was also going to see if Johnnie could defang the serpent by locking him out of all access to his bank accounts.

Harold had just finished dinner and was getting ready to sit down and do some reading when Alex called him. He was amazed at what she told had just happened. He asked what she wanted him to do. He readily agreed to raid the Mafia leader's home.

He would have an arrest and search warrant in his hands before midnight and he and his team and a sufficient number backup would raid the luxury apartment before sunrise.

He heard the sirens and asked that he be put in contact with whomever was in charge of the arriving police.

Alex said she was putting the phone down with the guns so she would not be accidently shot.

The arriving police all exited their cars with guns drawn and rushed forward.

Both she and Trey held up their open hands and identified themselves as police officers that worked for the Lieutenant Governor.

Alex was relieved when the person that seemed to be in charge had all the officers put away their weapons.

He came forward and looked at her and Trey's badges and asked what had happened.

Alex pointed to the phone next to her weapon and said that the area DEA leader wanted to have a word with him and was waiting on the phone.

She stepped back and watched as the conversation took place.

It was clear to her that Harold was exerting his influence by the way the officer was shaking his head in agreement.

He hung up and came over to her and said that her reputation was well known but that he had never expected to meet her.

He said that he had watched the burning barrage for hours until it sunk and not long after he had been on the investigating team when a shooter had tried to kill her when she had family and friends out fishing.

Alex took his offered hand, shook it, and thanked him for being one of the brave doing his job.

He suggested that she go in and relax while his men processed the scene. He pointed at the two guns on the hood of the car and asked if they were the weapons used to shoot the two men on the ground.

Alex nodded and said that they were and that she need to arrange for replacement weapons because her case was only on its first day.

She led the way back into the house and went out to the pool area where her mother and father were sitting.

She smiled and said that she had forgotten what had been on the menu for desert.

Rose-Anne laughed and said that she had forgotten about dessert. She then said that it was lemon meringue and a scoop of lemon ice cream on the side.

Alex said she would love a nice sized slice, and she would get a cup of iced tea to accompany it. She asked Trey if he wanted some iced tea.

Trey loved the way that Alex was able to step away from a harrowing experience and flow into what seemed like a very normal mode.

He knew why he was so devoted to his work partner. She not only was unbelievably brave, but she was unbelievably a people person who exuded a warmth that capture those around her.

Alex returned with two ice teas each with a lemon wedge on the edge of the glass.

She sat down and said she needed to call Johnnie and ask him to arrange it so Adriano would be unable to get to any of his money.

Johnnie was not surprised to get a call from Alex. He was very surprised when she shared what had just happened. He said he would be able to quickly change all the passwords to all the accounts that Adriano and the mafia headquarters had. He let her know that everything would happen in less than a half hour since he had already hacked into all the banks, and it would only be a matter of changing the passwords.

Alex thanked him and said that he had earned another tray of cookies.

She looked at Trey and said that it was great to be supported by the best.

Trey smiled and said that he was only second best because he could not shoot out the gun target's bullseye blind folded.

Alex laughed and said that she noticed that all his shots counted when they need to.

6 Smoking Gun

Adriano arrived at his apartment building and thanked the driver, walked over to the elevator, got on and pressed the button for his floor. He looked at himself in the polished stainless steel of the elevator wall and felt pleased with the tall, slender, thin faced man with black eyes, distinctive cheek, what he thought was a strong chin, a well tapered nose and black hair that was combed back on the sides and back across the top.

The door opened and he step out into an entry foyer. His one bedroom, three thousand square foot apartment took up two thirds of the floor and was situated to the lake side of the floor he was on. There was a small fifteen hundred square one bedroom apartment to his right currently occupied by a rich widow that had live there since the building opened.

He was in the second year of a ten-year lease. He opened the door with the Ap on his phone and walked into the bright white twenty-foot white entry area with white walls that ran one third of the way toward the lake.

To his left was a miniature statue of the thinker, that he had imported from Italy. It was highlighted by a spot light located at the top of the ten-foot ceiling.

The lighting of the foyer was an indirect light reflected off the ceiling from two light strips located about eight feet off the floor and hidden behind an angled shield.

He always felt as if he was home when he entered. The apartment had the smell he associated with it being new. He made sure that his cleaner kept it smelling that way.

Once in he hung his light jacket in an old closet that he had also brought from Italy that felt out of place but that anchored him to the feeling of his Sicilian roots he walked to the first hallway to his right and as he turned to go to his bedroom, he put his wallet in the alcove that he had built into the wall. This was where there was a key hanging that was for his antique Italian convertible sports car that was parked in the apartment's basement area. He hung up his key ring with the keys to his office and an assortment of keys that he used at work or elsewhere on a second hook.

As he walked toward his bedroom door, the kitchen was to his left and to his right was the area he considered his morning and evening personal relaxation area. It was where he read the paper in the morning and in the evening, he sat and watched the news and then watched two of his favorite early evening shows.

The kitchen to his left had a great view of the lake and when he did cook, he enjoyed the fact that the arrangement allowed him to look out to the lake while he was standing behind the stove. The area to the front of the kitchen was where he sat to enjoy a cup of coffee or tea and just take in the activity out on the lake or the people walking along the beach.

The bedroom was in the middle of the next section of the apartment. To the right was a large walk-in closet that took up one third of the width and there was a grand master bathroom that took up two thirds of the width of that section of the apartment.

The master bathroom featured a glass enclosed shower, a jacuzzi, a two-sink counter with a mirror that ran its length. He seldom used the Jacuzzi and was thinking about having it replaced with a powered swimming lane.

He changed into his exercise closes and walked out of the second door of his bedroom into the exercise area where there was a treadmill on the left, a stationary bike in the middle and a free weight area to the right. The front of the area was open to the lake side of the apartment so as he exercised, he again had a great view out across the lake.

The entire lake side of the apartment was surrounded by a floor to ceiling glass wall that went from the entry foyer around to the lake front and then back to the entrance of the exercise area.

The front of the apartment was an area that pulled you in and made you feel that you would be pulled out into the void beyond the glass. There were no curtains but there were sections that could be moved out to break up the feeling of being at risk of falling. He never used the panels except when he entertained a large group of people.

Once a month he would host his top leadership and their families and then he would have the panels positioned so that everyone could feel comfortable.

This was his treadmill exercise day and as he walked, he was thinking about the past weekend when he had driven in his convertible.

He always enjoyed getting the car ready to go out. He kept it in a dehumidified bubble that lifted directly up toward the ceiling. He would check the oil and other fluids and then turn on the engine. Next, he would make sure the tires were at the right pressure. He would clean the wind shield and the mirrors. Then he would put down the cover and wipe off the leather seats with a leather treatment.

He would then put away all the cleaning gear. He was then ready and drove slowly out of the garage.

He mostly drove the smaller highways and always stayed exactly at or just below the speed limit. He was not going to stress the car, and he did not want to get a traffic ticket. It amazed him that he was constantly getting honked at and given the finger of some irritated driver that would speed by.

He had gone out to a nature sanctuary where he liked to hike and fish. When using his car and going fishing, he always fished catch and release because he was not going to carry any fish in the car.

As he slowed down his pace on the treadmill, he looked at his phone to see what time it was. He had expected a call from his two enforcers before he had started, and he was now angry that they had not followed his instructions.

He had made them stand in his office and repeat his personal number until they could do it from memory because he did not want them to write it down or put it on their phone. He wondered if they could possibly have forgotten.

The apartment bell rang, and he looked at the security screen to see who it might be. He saw that it was his Chinese dinner being delivered. He instructed the person delivering it to put it on the stand to the side of the door. He had paid and given a good tip via that Ap that he had so that he did not have to open the door to some stranger. He waited until the person got on the elevator and then went out and brought the meal in.

He chose to sit at the table in front of the kitchen so he could enjoy the view of the lake.

The more he thought about his two assassins the angrier he got. He decided to put them aside and focus on relaxing and enjoying the view.

After cleaning up from dinner he decided to take a long shower and get a good night's sleep.

Harold had activated his team, contacted the judge to get both an arrest warrant and a search warrant.

He was now on the phone with Johnnie who was in Cincinnati. They were discussing how to get into the apartment where Adriano lived. Johnnie said that he would turn off the security system and when they got to the floor where Adriano resided, he would open the apartment door lock, and they could enter cautiously. He would also control the lighting.

The only sensitive part would be to go into the bedroom and arrest Adriano. Johnnie added that hopefully, he did not sleep with a loaded gun under his pillow.

Harold got Alex on the line and asked if she wanted to be part of the raid.

She responded that she would love to be present on the phone but not in person. She said that she preferred to be sipping on a hot cup of tea and listening in.

He agreed to have one of his team members to call her so that could happen.

Trey commented that he would be on line with Alex.

Mary-Anne asked what time the raid was going to take place.

Alex let her know that it would be four in the morning.

Mary-Anne walked out of the kitchen and returned shortly carrying a table top speaker phone that she said she used when having a conference and said that she would fix an early morning breakfast of rolls, toast and whatever else they might desire.

She said that the phone would be on mute, and they could pretend that they were listening to an old-time thriller being performed on the radio.

Alex laughed and said that she was not sure about the thriller part and hoped it would be rather dull.

She connect her phone to the speaker phone and made sure everything was on mute.

Then she suggested they all get some sleep and come down bright and early.

Marge was given the duty of connecting with Alex. She laughed and asked if she could drop her phone in the event that she had to pull her weapon to defend herself.

Harold shook his head and joked that she needed to keep Alex involved since she was a better shot.

He then said that it was time to get the team to the apartment building and set up in the basement parking area. He had Johnnie on the line and when they arrived at the apartment building, he asked Johnnie to open up the entrance gate and was surprised that almost immediately after asking the gate went up.

The team got out and he made sure the each was wearing their Kevlar outfits. He made sure everything was ready. He had put in his ear buds so that he could listen to Johnnie but keep everything as quiet as possible. He then went to the elevator and was once again surprised when it opened as he approached it. He heard Johnnie say that he had the way prepared.

When the door opened on the thirtieth, the lights dimmed, and Johnnie said that he had disabled the security system, and the apartment door was unlocked.

The team entered and the lights came up to a low level.

Johnnie described the way to the bedroom and added the bedroom door was unlocked and as far as he could tell the lights were off.

Harold had one of the team kneel to the side of the door and push it open. He stepped in and to the side. Johnnie turned the lights to a very low level.

The team entered and surrounded the bed.

Adriano remained sound asleep with an eye cover over his eyes.

Harold quietly asked Johnnie to turn the lights fully on throughout the entire apartment.

When the lights were on, he loudly called out for Adriano to raise his hands because he was under arrest

Adriano ripped his eye cover off and sat up right in bed. It was obvious that he was confused.

Harold then repeated his request that Adriano raise his hands because he was under arrest for the attempted murder of a law enforcement officer.

Adriano said he had no idea what he was being accused of. He asked if the entry to his apartment was legal.

Harold handed him the search warrant and the arrest warrant.

Harold instructed him to get dressed and he would be sure to explain the situation as he was taken to a holding cell until he could stand before a judge.

Adriano made the mistake of using the line, "do you know who you are dealing with."

The entire team laughed and said that indeed they did, and they figured scum came in all shapes and sizes.

Mary-Anne had been making toast and listening in. She yawned and commented that she should have slept in with Russel who had declined to get up early to be part of the raid.

Alex thanked Harold's team for taking her along and that she was signing off.

She later called Harold and got brought up to date to how he was handling the operation, and that the main mafia office was cordoned off and an investigative team was going through it tooth and nail. They had already found the gun storage area where a huge arsenal of weapons were stored and had linked the ammunition there to the ammunition used by the two gunmen at her home.

They had the smoking gun, and it would be useful, but he said that the best weapon that would most likely to send Adriano to prison was as old as what had been used in the age of prohibition. It was the tax evasion information that Johnnie had guided the team to.

6 Smoking Gun

7 Introduction

*A*lex and Trey were talking about the fact that they were about to hit the twenty-four-hour mark of how long they had been in Chicago but that it seemed more like a month.

Trey shook his head and said that he thought that their world had gone into hyperdrive, and it was hard to fathom what had happened. He looked at Alex and commented that he really admired how she had immediately launched a counter attack to the unbelievable attack they had survived.

He then said that he also appreciated the fact that her father had realized he had a dangerous daughter and had built a four-gauge shotgun, slug proof door that had given them a chance to take the two assassins down.

Alex laughed and said that they should give her dad an award for that door. She wished she had been around to see how he handled making the door. She said that she wondered what he had to do to reinforce the frame to hold the door.

They arrived at the apartment building and were guided to the area where Adriano's prize antique Italian sports car was parked. Alex walked over and looked at the dark plastic bubble and asked if she could see how it worked. She took a series of pictures as the officer in charge pressed a button that caused the plastic cover to be lifted up. Alex took another series of pictures. She asked if the cover was custom made or if it was a specific brand name.

The officer pointed to a small emblem on the control panel. Alex walked over, read "Covers for Lovers.com," and took a picture of it. She said that she thought that her Jag should have something similar.

Trey laughed and said that the cover would most likely cost more than the Jag. Besides, she had a father that was constantly making certain that her Jag was in super shape.

Alex nodded and said that he was probably right, but she was going to check it out anyway. She then pointed to the Jag and said it was time to go and greet Adriano at his new residence.

When they arrived at the police headquarters where Harold had said Adriano was being held until his arraignment, after both showed their credentials, they were guided into the parking area.

Harold was standing up on the walkway waiting for them. He had two individuals standing with him that were in very formal-looking black suits, and both sported very nice leather brief cases. The only difference between the two was that the person that was a sandy blond had a light brown brief case and the one with black hair had a black briefcase.

Harold introduce brown briefcase as Andy Weller who was the IRS lawyer and black briefcase as Lenord Maxwell who was a criminal lawyer and a partner in the Maxwell Family Law Practice.

Alex greeted both of them and introduced herself and Trey as special agents currently working for the Illinois Lieutenant governor.

Harold said that he had arranged that they got to see and talk with Adriano before he called his lawyer. He had been made aware that Adriano had a lawyer that he insisted he get to call.

Alex stopped and asked that she be given ten minutes before she met with Adriano. She pulled Trey aside and said that she needed to talk with Johnnie because she had figured out a way to move Adriano into a tighter net.

She dialed Johnnie and asked him if he could do what Kekoa had done with the billionaire bank accounts.

Johnnie said he understood her request and he would immediately make a few key changes that would handle her immediate need and then he would contact Kekoa and take some lessons from him and organize everything the way that Kekoa had organized the material for the IRS.

Alex thanked him and then rejoined Harold. She let Andy know that he would get all the details that would let him track the money, get to the banks and to the accounts where the money was held. These banks would be in the US and offshore.

He would have that information by the time that Adriano was brought to court to be charged for money laundering and failure to pay taxes.

Andy asked how she could possibly do that in the next twenty-four hours.

Alex smiled and responded because she had a wizard whose magic supported her.

Harold asked who should take the lead when they met with Adriano.

She looked at Lenord, smile and said that he had the tougher case, and she was counting on he and his law firm to pile on and put Adriano in prison for the attempted murder of two law officers. She added that he might be acquainted with her mother who would be quite willing to help his law firm.

Lenord nodded and said that he was quiet familiar with her mother's reputation and would be sure to reach out to her.

Alex then said that she would appreciate taking the lead.

They were led to a meeting room where they were asked to sit on one side of the room. A moment later, Adriano, wearing an orange coverall and wearing white sneakers was led in. His handcuffs were connected to a ring on the table.

It was clear that he was upset and asked why he had not been allowed to call his lawyer.

Alex smiled and replied because she first wanted to introduce herself. She added that she had come to Chicago with peaceful intensions but had instead faced a chilling greeting colder than the wind from the lake on a cold winter's day.

She added that she was the person that he had tried to have assassinated three times. She then pointed to Leonard Maxwell and said that he would charge him with the attempted murder of two police officers. She added that those charges would keep him in court for at least five years followed by life in prison unless he were given the death penalty.

She went on to introduce Andy Weller the Chicago region IRS leader, who would charge him with money laundering and failure to pay taxes. Given scope of the number of bank accounts he managed, the result would be least thirty years in prison.

Finally, you have met Harold Zimmerman who with his team woke you up bright and early this morning and brought you to enjoy your orange outfit and she added that she was sure a very healthy morning meal. She then stated that the DEA would bringing charges of possessing illegal weapons. This would be the least of the charges but one that carried a fifteen-year penalty.

The final person who she introduced was Trey as the person who always had her back, and she pointed out that he had no one that was going to come forward to have his back. She added that his organization will tell you to be a good boy and face the music.

Now that I have made all the introductions let me tell you that you had better let your organization know that the Chicago Mafia is without its top leader and that you will be out of circulation for most of the rest of your lifetime.

Adriano looked at Alex and almost shouted that she had no idea how powerful he was and how soon he would be out and this time he would not fail.

Alex nodded and as she stood to leave, she said that he could now have his one phone call. She turned and everyone left with her.

After leaving the room Harold looked at her and said that was the most satisfying meeting that he had ever attended.

Andy thanked her for doing what she had just done. He was now really looking forward to getting the information that would make sure that Adriano was kept in jail for the entire time the case went on.

Lenord asked if her mother was as tough a nut as she was.

Alex smiled and replied that she was the softy as compared to her mother.

Lenord said that the first meeting he was planning to have after getting everyone in his practice up to speed was to meet with her mother.

Alex then invited the three go out on a weekend fishing trip that she was hosting. She looked at Harold and made sure he understood that it was he, his team, and all significant others.

On the way to the car, Trey said he was ready for his nap. Alex agreed and asked if later he wanted to go with her to the harbor and arrange for a weekend excursion on the Golden Goose. She also wanted to swing by the Pizzeria and arrange to have the event catered.

Trey said that sounded like a good plan otherwise he would spend the day in bed and not be able to sleep that night.

Alex said that after the previous night she figured she would have no trouble sleeping.

As she looked ahead to the house and saw that it was clear. The crime scene had been cleaned up and the bodies were gone, and the blood had been washed away. The roses were back where they had originally been. The only thing that remained visible was a shiny spot in the middle of the front door where the slug from the four-gauge slug had hit.

Alex parked in the garage and commented that her Jag had a very nice place to sit while she was away and that the cover over like the one Adriano had over his convertible was an over kill.

She walked back to the front door and put her finger in the hole that the slug had made. It was the only imperfection in an otherwise beautiful front door. She now took notice of the heavy-duty cement frame that supported the door. She stepped back and took a picture of it.

She wondered how much the door had cost her father.

Dexter was lounging behind the counter glad that it was a slow Thursday. He looked up, smiled, walked around the counter, and gave Alex a hug. He asked when she was going to host another of her famous fishing trips.

Alex laughed and said that was the reason she had come to him. She asked if Saturday would be possible.

Dexter said that the Golden Goose was ready to go out any time Alex wanted her to do so. He asked how many people would be going out so he could get everything ready.

She stopped to count and then replied that there would be twenty-five people.

He asked about children.

Alex smiled and said it would be the same three young people who were now no longer children.

She then shared some of the details of what had happened the previous day at her parents' home. She showed him the picture of the door that she credited with saving all of them. She added that her father had built the door after the two fishing trips that she had taken out on the lake. He told her that those outings had caused him to anticipate that his daughter might attract someone that might want to break in.

She said she had a picture of her father pointing to something and the picture of the door with the shiny spot where the slug had hit. She wondered if he might know someone who could merge the two picture, print it and frame it.

Dexter nodded and said that he could sent the pictures to the person who mounted the fish for his guests, and he was sure that in a day he could get it delivered and have it on the Golden Goose.

Alex thanked him. Then she added that she wanted to connect him with her mother's pizzeria and let him arrange the catering and food for the fishing outing. Lunch was to be out on the lake, but dinner would be at her house, and he was invited to come as well.

She realized that she needed to call the two people she worked for and give them a first-hand report of what had transpired in the last twenty-four hours. It was to her a twenty-four-hour period that seem more like twenty-four months.

She drove to the Evercrest Pizzeria and walked in to greet her first police boss, Jason Shepard, who was now running the pizza shop.

He stopped what he was doing and came out from behind the counter to give her a hug. He asked what she was up to.

She said that if he came out fishing, he would get the scoop on what had happened in the last twenty-four hours.

He laughed and said that he would love to go fishing as long as a gun battle was not part of the trip.

Alex smiled and said that she did not think that would happen, but gun battles seemed to follow her footsteps.

She asked if she could have a plain cheese pizza with extra cheese.

<u>*8 Sent to the Closet*</u>

*A*driano could hardly contain himself as he watched the Black witch head out the door. He now had one goal in mind and that was to get released and have every person he had at his disposal assigned to eliminate her.

He made the phone call to his lawyer. He was confident that he would be able to manipulate the system and get him out on bail.

He made sure that it was understood that a substantial bonus on top of the normal fees was to be had.

The discussion of the charges led his lawyer to comment that they were not in a very good position. There were at least four major charges and depending on how the IRS split the cases it might be as many as ten separate charges.

He went on to say that the most damming charges that would keep him from getting bail were the three assassination attempts of a police officer.

Adriano was not pleased with what he was told. He needed to get out so he could leverage the people in his organization.

After his lawyer left, Adriano decided that there should be a fourth assassination attempt. He had a person on the police swat team that was a sniper and who was on his payroll. She had impressed him the day he had interviewed her. She had been on the payroll of his predecessor. Since his arrival he had continued to pay her five thousand a month to stand by and be available when needed. He figured that it was now the time that she was needed.

He was able to activate her by communicating through one of his field lieutenants who gave her the information needed for her to carry out the assassination.

This time he hoped that the assassin would succeed.

When Olivia received the order, she at first panicked. Then she realized that she had the opportunity to come out of the cold. She had been under cover for most of her police career. She wanted to get back to a normal life. She talked it over with her contact that worked in the Lieutenant Governor's office and got support for getting herself killed.

She would then be transferred to another police district and get back to having a real life. She was still young enough to have children and planned to do so with or without a significant other.

Her world was about to change for the better.

Jane shook her head as she thought about the situation. She had an undercover policewoman working for her that was supposed to off a special investigator that also reported to her who was going to kill the policewoman.

She had yet to hear from Alex, her special investigator. She had talked to Harold, her friend in the DEA and knew what had transpired the night before and the follow-up apprehension of the Chicago Mafia leader.

As if she had willed a call from her special investigator, Alex was at the other end of the line when she answered her next call.

Alex shared the fact that she was late in calling but it seemed that events had transpired so fast that she had trouble keeping up.

Jane let her know that she had talked to Harold and knew the details where he was directly involved but he only knew second hand what had happened at Alex's parents' the house.

Alex gave her an update about what had happened and the fact that she and Trey had killed the two men sent to kill them.

Jane then explained the situation that had come up because Adriano had ordered another assassination. She shared the fact that she had an undercover sniper on the swat team that also worked for the Mafia. She had received orders to shoot and kill Alex.

Alex asked how they should handle this new situation.

Jane said that her undercover agent wanted to get killed so she could return to a normal life.

Alex suggested that an attempt at the pier, or one out on the water as the Golden Goose went out as two potential spots. From a small boat out on the water, the person in the boat could get hit, fall over board and disappear below the water.

Jane said that the small boat scene offered the best way for it to take place. She would have her team set up the situation. The only other thing that needed to happen was that the scene be captured, and that it all seemed real.

Alex said that she would handle making it all seem real and getting it captured so it would make the evening news.

After hanging up she called the Chief and brought him up to date.

The Chief said that Johnnie had been giving everyone in Cincinnati a running commentary of what had gone on, so they were all up to date and everyone was eager to go fishing.

Alex did not tell him about another assassination attempt.

Alex said that breakfast would be available on board the Golden Goose bright and early and that it would leave harbor on time at eight.

The Chief said that they would all be there.

Alex spent the evening getting her props ready. Both her and Trey's issued weapons were being held in evidence, so she had cleaned and prepared her personal pistol that she used for target practice. She went out in the garage and loaded some bullets and put wax heads on them.

She selected one of her older blouses and cut a small hole in the middle of her chest then she used a piece of tape to hold the hole closed.

She modified her Kevlar vest so that she could wear it under her blouse and were the hole in the blouse was located she positioned a flattened bullet by using two-sided tape to hold it in place.

The only person she shared what she was doing was Trey. He would film everything that was happening. Then when she was hit and knelt down, he was to pull the flattened bullet off the vest and hold it up for everyone to see. The two of them would take the dingy out to where the shooters boat was located and when they got there, they would signal back that the shooter was dead.

Then they would standby as a police boat came speeding out to take control of the scene. He should film the dead body being pulled out of the water and then stop filming.

She had sent Jane a text saying that her killer was to stand to take her shot and then when Alex raised her gun and fired twice, she was to fall backward into the water and stay behind the boat. She let Jane know that she had arranged for some local police friends to come out by boat and pull the body of the shooter from the water and zip her into a body bag.

After she got off the call, Trey commented that he would drive to the airport on Friday afternoon to pick up Lindsey and Nolan and bring them back to the house.

Alex suggested that she hire her personal cabby to meet them and drive them up.

Trey said that that felt like a great relief. He was still trying to recover from their Wednesday right and then their early morning participation in the arrest which was followed by going to the jail where Adriano was being held.

Alex suggested they relax by the pool and watch her mother busily making various snacks for the early evening get together.

Rose-Anne marveled that her daughter and Trey seemed so relaxed after having been involved in an assassination attempt and then having the Mafia boss arrested.

She had been contacted by the firm that was to prosecute the case against the Mafia boss and had agreed to meet with them after the week end.

Alex had let her know that one of the partners of the firm would be going fishing with them. She had laughed and said that her daughter was setting things up for her and thanked her.

Alex shook her head and said that setting her up had never crossed her mind. Harold was the person who had brought in that specific law firm. She pointed out that the local IRS had also been pulled in by Harold and he would also be going out with them.

She then reminded her that everyone going out would be coming to dinner after the fishing trip.

Rose-Anne said that one of the main dishes would be the fish that was caught but she also had Jason were working with a local caterer to have lobster tail, spare ribs, rib eye, prime rib, and a variety of sides such as butter milk biscuits, creamed spinach, delicata squash and twice baked sweet potatoes catered in.

Alex asked what she had in mind for desert.

Rose-Anne said that she had several deserts in mind such as, Baked Peaches, Strawberry Tart, Espresso Martini Ice Cream without the Martini, Chocolate Covered Strawberries, and a variety of ice cream flavors. She was leaving it up to the caterers based on what was available locally.

Alex said that it would be hard for her to control herself when it came to the deserts, and it would cost her hours on the treadmill.

Lindsey arrived from the airport and Anni came with her. Nolan, Linda, and Laurie ran to her and gave her a hug. Brian and Kekoa, and Anela had all flown up on the same flight.

Brian commented that he had never seen anyone that was as fast as she was at arresting the person who had tried to have her killed.

Alex was pleased to see them all and said they should gather around the pool area. She said that in a few moments her mother's Pizzeria would deliver several variety of pizzas and a wide variety of snacks such as bruschetta, meatballs, buffalo wings, honey BBQ wings, plain and spicy onion rings, zucchini fries, antipasto salad and garlic bread.

She pointed to the pool side refrigerator and said that it was loaded with a variety of soft drinks.

The chatter and laughter filled that pool side area. The food arrived and everyone dug in and continued the evening celebration.

About nine thirty, Alex suggested that those that were staying should make sure they were ready for bed and those that needed to get to the hotel should do so because it was going to be an early morning.

She said that she was calling it a day and going up to her room so she would be ready the next day.

Trey commented that he was still trying to get over the hours his work partner made him work and he was going to go up to his room as well.

Lindsey could see that Trey and Alex both looked exhausted, and she signaled Nolan that it was time to say goodnight.

Annie signaled to Brian that it was time for them to go to the hotel.

The evening ended and the cleaning crew from the pizzeria went into action and less than an hour later it would have been hard to believe that a major gathering had broken up.

Rose-Anne thanked Jason for having arranged for the food and the help in such a short time. She remined him that he was to come out fishing.

Back in her apartment Olivia was getting ready to get some sleep as well. She had driven out to where she was to be fishing and had rented a boat at the marina. She had been instructed to rent the boat from a small concern that was across the harbor from where the Golden Goose was tied off. She was impressed with the beauty of the yacht and wished she were going out on it instead of the boat she was to die on.

She cleaned her sniper's rifle and put it in its carrying case and then in the trunk of her car.

It took her forever to get to sleep, and it seemed that her alarm woke her up immediately afterwards.

The drive to the marina in the dark seemed an appropriate setting. She kept going over the upcoming shooting that would free her to live a normal life.

She had made sure she had no live ammo and that the one shot she would take was a wax head cap.

She knew that her actions had to be believable.

Everyone needed to believe she was dead.

9 Another Sniper's Death

*A*lex was up by five getting ready for what she hoped would be a believable performance of getting shot and of killing a would-be assassin. She had modified her Kevlar pullover so that it was short sleeve and hidden under her blouse that had the strategic hole at the center of her breast. She made sure that everything was as it should be then she drove to the boat harbor. Before going out to the Golden Goose she met with the local police team that would come out to pick up the body of the supposedly dead undercover policewoman who had been asked by Adriano to kill her. Alex thought through the very complicated and delicate performance that she and the person doing the assassination were undertaking. It had to be good enough to convince what would most likely be at least a local news cast audience.

After having agreed on the pickup teams actions and her actions, she walked out to the Golden Goose and put her personal items on board and then walked up to the bait house.

She saw the lights come on just as she reached the end of the pier. She walked in and said good morning to Dexter who was just getting ready to carry a bait bucket and a bait box out to the Golden Goose.

He asked why she was so early.

She said that she had come to make sure that everything was ready on such short notice and that the group had grown by a few people.

Dexter nodded and said that he could handle a dozen more if necessary.

Alex replied that it would perhaps be only a couple.

She followed as he carried the bait bucket and picked up two more poles.

Once on board, he turned on the engine.

He asked if she would like a couple of pancakes for breakfast.

Alex smiled and said that she would love a couple and if possible two over easy eggs on top and a ton of syrup.

She was sitting out on the deck as the sun rose in a splendor of red, orange, and yellow splashing along the bottom of the few cumulus clouds that were floating slowly across the lake towards her. She saw her father park the large conversion van next to her Jag.

She laughed as everyone inside seemed to come out like clowns in a circus who come out of a tiny car in a continuous stream that seems to go on forever.

She counted nine people in total. Then another van arrived and the Chief, his wife, Bill, his wife, Trever, his wife, Johnnie, and Mary all got out.

Seventeen people were all talking and laughing as they walked down the pier. She knew that Harold and his wife, and his team members and their spouses had yet to arrive, and they would add another eight people. It came to her that she had invited the lawyer and the IRS agents and that added four more. She then saw Jason and his wife arrive. That meant that if she counted herself and Dexter there would be thirty-three people on board.

She checked with Dexter who said that it would be crowded but that it would be no problem, and he had plenty of food coming and that there would be two caterers going out with them as well.

Alex thought through the performance that she had coming up and decided that she should take one of the rear fishing spots so that most of the people were behind her as the Golden Goose left the harbor.

After everyone was on board and had time to grab a breakfast box and find a place where they would fish Dexter declared that it was time to cast off.

She had a fishing box that held her gun next to her and had her pole leaning against the back deck rail as Dexter pulled away from the pier and headed out to the lake.

Alex saw the boat with the would-be assassin sitting exactly where she figured it would be. She looked back and saw the pick-up team putting their thirty-foot police boat into the water. It was now almost time for the spot light to be on her and she hoped that her performance would be believable.

She stood acting as if she were preparing her pole. She glanced around and saw that Trey was in position with his phone in hand.

She had just turned back when she saw the would-be assassin stand up and raise her rifle. Alex counted one and then fell to her knees, pulled her blouse so that the hole would appear. She opened her fishing box, pulled out her weapon, stood up, aimed, and shot three times. She watched as the shooter dropped her weapon into the boat and fell backwards into the water.

Trey rushed up, as if to check on her and she pulled a flattened slug from the hole in her blouse and handed it to him. She noted that Trey had his camera filming the entire time. She knew that she would later praise his focus on capturing the scene.

She took note that Dexter had stopped the Golden Goose.

She jumped up and said that they needed to get to the boat to make sure the shooter was dead. She rushed to where the Golden Goose's dingy was secured, dropped it into the water and she and Trey jumped in. They sped toward the dingy as she made a loud call for backup. It was a call that went nowhere and was done so it was heard by Trey's recording.

They got to the fishing boat, took a picture of the inside of the boat where the sniper's rifle lay and then took a picture of the shooter lying face down in the water with a dark circle of blood encircling it.

Then the sirens of the police boat caused them to pan the camera around to an oncoming boat speeding toward them. Alex put her hand with her gun in it up in the air as the spotlight on the boat focused on her. She made a production of putting the gun down. And shouting out that she was police.

The boat slowed and pulled along the other side of the fishing boat and with a pole pulled the "body" to its side. Two of the officers pulled the body out of the water. They made sure that the body had its back to the camera as it was pulled on board and then placed in a body bag. Only the zipping action was visible.

They then came around and had Alex put her gun in an evidence bag. And made a point of verifying her and Trey's badge ids.

When asked where she was going to be so they could follow up with her and return her weapon, she pointed to the Golden Goose and said that she was on the way to go fishing for most of the day.

They asked if she would come to the station once she was back and she agreed.

Trey quit recording the scene at that point and they returned to the Golden Goose.

The Chief watched the entire event and as Alex and Trey were returning, he felt like going to the back rail and clapping for one of the best performances that he had ever watched. He hoped that it was a good enough performance and be as good as what Alex wanted.

Alex wanted to ask someone if it were good enough but there would not be a second take it was good enough or it was a bust. She told Trey to release it to the news networks.

She went in and changed out of her blouse and put on a T shirt that boasted that she had caught the big fish. This was the T shirt that she had bought to celebrate her and Matt's relationship.

Dexter guided the Golden Goose out to where he normally went and then put it adrift out where the fishing was usually excellent.

It was hard for Alex to concentrate on fishing. After catching one nice trout she put her pole away. She filled a plate with vegetables snacks, got herself a large-iced tea and sat down at the table in the middle of the deck.

She wished that Matt had been able to come up for the weekend, but his team had been short of people, and at the last moment he ended up staying in Cincinnati.

The Chief came and sat down with her and congratulated her on her excellent shooting. He added that it was very lucky that she had worn her Kevlar protection to go fishing.

Alex knew that she had not fooled the Chief and that he was letting her know. She replied that after three assassination attempts on her she figured that she should be extra cautious. She then added that she would have to bring him up to speed on all the details when they had a chance to talk in private.

The Chief nodded and said that he would make himself available as soon as possible. He was wondering why he had been left out of the loop.

Trey came over to the table and said that three local news stations were sending their crews to interview her when they returned to the Harbor.

Alex groaned and said that she would try to enjoy the rest of the time out fishing so that she had enough energy to face the questioning she would be taking.

The Chief suggested that he and Harold get between her and the newscasters and field the questions.

Alex smiled and said that if he were Johnnie, she would make him two trays of cookies.

Johnnie had been fishing close by and had heard the exchange and said she should not be giving away his trays of cookies which he felt he had earned on this assignment.

Alex laughed and replied that when she got back to Cincinnati, she would just cook up a storm and bake a dozen trays of cookies.

The Chief got up and walked over to where Harold was fishing. He got his agreement to face the media and then went to get a brat. He had figured out that Alex needed everyone on board to believe the staged scene was real and the less everyone knew the more likely it would be believed.

Alex decided that the seat at the kitchen area table would be more comfortable. She was happy to see that the condiments and extra boxes of food had been put on the table and that no one was sitting where she wanted to sit. She slid in and was soon asleep.

The crew on the police boat turned to return to the harbor. Olivia got up and thanked them for getting her out of the freezing cold water. One of the crew laughed and said that the cold water helped to preserve dead bodies. He handed her a blanket and asked if they had come fast enough.

She said that yes, they had, and she was happy about the prospect of coming in from the cold.

He said that he would be glad to help her in her transition back to a normal life and would be happy to take her out to dinner whenever she was ready.

Olivia smiled and said that she would be happy to accept his invitation once she was free to do so. She was already happy about her return to the normal world. She spent the afternoon at a local pizzeria chatting with her new friend.

She received instructions to report for work at a police station in Waukegan. She was to leave her car where she had parked it and go by bus to her new apartment. Once again, she felt alive.

Alex came awake when the vibration of the engine of the Golden Goose let her know that Dexter was taking her back to the harbor.

She walked back out onto the deck. Her mother came over to her and asked how her nap had been.

The news crews at the head of the pier had each positioned their cameramen and interviewers and were ready to focus on the Black detective. The stations had done the initial investigations and knew that she was a top Cincinnati detective that was on special assignment with the office of the Illinois Lieutenant Governor.

They geared up their repertoire as the yacht approached the pier.

Alex waited as everyone disembarked. She was making it a point to be among the last to get off.

The Chief took the lead and walked toward the maze of the news crews. He knew exactly how to handle the situation.

Alex had been in similar situations and knew that the Chief and Harold would do the lead in. She would step forward, introduce Trey, and then answer about a dozen questions after which the Chief would step forward and close the interviewing down.

It went exactly as she figured it would.

Everyone else had left. The Chief and Harold went to where Harold's team was waiting.

She and Trey went to her Jag and then drove back to the house together. She complemented him on being an excellent cameraman.

Trey laughed and said he had a lot of practice doing selfies with Nolan and Lindsey.

He asked if she thought that the video was good enough to pull off their subterfuge.

Alex nodded and said that she hoped for Olivia's sake it was.

On his trip to the cafeteria, Adriano saw the news cast of the assassination attempt and the news interview. He was in disbelief as he absentmindedly poked at his meat loaf and mashed potato. She had survived four attempts and had killed three of the people that he had assigned to assassinate her. He was sure she had orchestrated his arrest and set up the charges he faced.

He figured it was time to see if he could bribe his way out of his current predicament. He also planned to seek help from his bosses back in Italy.

His lawyers successfully delayed the addition of a third charge of attempting to kill an officer of the law. He was informed that the charge would likely be added when the details of the incident were presented to the judge.

Adriano received additional bad news when his Italian bosses told him that he should face the charges and when it was clear what his fate was to be they would get back to him about his options.

For the first time in his career, he came to realize that he had lost control of the situation around him. He now realized that he should have listened to his leadership team about leaving the Cincinnati detective alone.

He was further dismayed when his second in his Chicago leadership team was promoted to run the Chicago organization.

It was then that he realized what it felt to be at the bottom of the barrel. The fact that he was still alive was the only bright spot in his very disturbed mind.

Alex and Trey arrived at the house to find everyone out by the pool enjoying each other's stories about the fish that they caught or the one that had gotten away.

They were both surrounded and had to answer a ton of question about what had happened. Her mother came to the rescue and said that she needed Alex in the kitchen for a moment.

Alex followed her mother and when they got to the kitchen her mother said that she was just a front for the Chief and the DEA, who were waiting in the library.

Alex thanked her and took a glass of iced tea and walked back to the library.

The Chief greeted her, held up a golf trophy, and presented her with the best actress of the year award.

Harold clapped said that the award would also be enriched with an around the world tour.

Alex smiled and admitted that it had been a staged shooting in order to give a long-time undercover operative the opportunity to come out of the cold. This operative, who was now turning thirty-five, had been undercover as a sniper assassin for the mafia for seven years. For the first time, she had been activated by the Mafia chief to perform an assassination. She needed her dying to be as real as possible.

The Chief smiled and said that he was proud of her and that he felt that she had pulled it off. He had watched the news reports and felt that the footage that Trey had shot, and released anonymously, had done the job.

Alex smiled and said that the only thing that it had cost her was the loss of an old blouse and the fact that she would have to buy a replacement for the top half of her Kevlar suit. She added that she was currently weaponless because her officially assigned weapon and her personal weapon were both being held as evidence.

The Chief laughed and said that since she had quit being issued new cars that had all been destroyed by her attackers, he now had money in his budget to replace her weapons. He said she should put in her order for a new weapon.

Alex gave him a hug and whispered that the one she had in mind would only cost a few thousand.

10 Unseen Spirit

Adriano's time in his cell seemed endless. He had never spent so much time doing absolutely nothing. He paced around in his cell but that only seemed to make things worse. Once a day he was taken out to a fenced in courtyard and allowed an hour to walk around or do whatever pleased him. He usually walked, did a few pushups, squats, knee bends and sit ups on the well-worn bench that was in the courtyard. He realized that he had lost track of the number of days that he had been in confinement. He felt certain that it was beyond the legal time, and he was going to have his lawyer put in an objection about the amount of time.

His lawyer had let him know that the time was not excessive. She had also been surprised that the IRS had a very detailed accounting of the money flow, the amounts and how they were moved through specific banks to launder the money. She also became aware about how many of the details she was unfamiliar with.

She had reviewed everything with various lawyers in the firm and they each privately said that her client's goose was cooked.

She kept that fact from Adriano because she knew it would infuriate him, and he would want her to take actions that were illegal.

After a week of waiting, Adriano was ready for any action, getting taken to court seemed to release his negative feelings. He had been allowed to dress in one of his expensive Italian black suits and he was wearing one of his impeccable polished pairs of black shoes. Except for being handcuffed, he felt human once again.

Two policemen escorted him into the courtroom. He looked around and was surprised to see that Alex Evercrest was not there. He had figured she would be present at the prosecution table or sitting behind it, but she was clearly not in the room.

He took another look.

His surprise affected him mentally because he had been so sure she would be there to gloat at his predicament. She was not there but he felt her presence. He did not believe in spirits but in this case, he was sure that her spirit was present and that it might even be laughing at him. He now thought of her as a shadow fighter.

He sat down with his lawyer and took in the other people in the courtroom. His second in command who had been promoted to take his place was not there but two of his leadership team were sitting in the back. This made sense to him since it would be a bad idea for the new mafia chief to be present at the trial.

The judge entered and all rose and waited for his order to be seated.

The judge turned to the prosecution and asked him what the charges against the defendant were.

The prosecution rose and detailed the charge of tax evasion and money laundering and sat down.

This was a surprise to the defense. The judge knew what he was walking into the room to preside over.

The defense had been prepared to declare innocence to the charge of attempted murder. She had been aware of the charge of money laundering and tax evasion but was surprised that it was the charge that the prosecution had decided to prosecute first. She had been sure that the more serious crime would be first.

She rose and let the judge know that her client was pleading not guilty to the charges.

She knew that he was guilty as sin, but her job was to defend him, and she hoped that she could somehow guide the trial so that she could get the minimum for those charges.

She knew that she would have her hands full during jury selection trying to identify jurors that would be amiable to the idea of not paying taxes.

It would be harder to select them based on the millions of dollars involved in the money laundering scheme. It would be cheating on taxes versus on moving millions of illegally gained money to make it look as if it were legal.

She wished she had gone to work for a law firm that was not so closely connected to the Mafia. The firm was always skirting the illegal side but stayed just inside the legal part of the laws that they were dealing with.

She now wondered when and how the sledge hammer of the charges for attempted murder would hit. It was clear to her that the prosecution strategy was to prosecute the case that could quickly move forward and be resolved and then bring up the more complicated case.

She wondered how long she had while the prosecution hunted down bank accounts and where and when money had been moved in order for it to prove the money laundering part of the trial.

She was to be surprised by the fact that it would take less than a month.

Alex had returned to Cincinnati. She, Trey, Bill, Trevor, Johnnie, and the Chief were all sitting in a team room watching the opening session.

Johnnie had tapped into the courts video cameras and was moving from view to view that gave the rather dry proceedings some life. He was also providing some humorous dialogue about what Adriano was thinking.

It was clear by the dialogue in the room that everyone was enjoying the session.

They all would have been surprised at the accuracy of Johnnies' dialogue about the fact that Alex was not present as Adriano walked in and looked around several times.

Alex laughed and said that she had taken Brian's and Kekoa's advice to give the spot light to the IRS and the court lawyers and fade from the scene. She added that she had decided that she needed time to bake the cookies she had promised because she knew she would be held accountable to deliver the cookies as promised.

Johnnie held up one of her cookies and replied that it was great that they got to see the kickoff of the trial while enjoying some of those cookies.

Alex nodded and said that she hoped that replacing Adriano would end the pointless revenge attitude that he had exhibited.

The Chief added that he could now focus on what Cincinnati needed from his detectives.

Bill added that he too was ready to focus on the issues the area faced.

Trevor shook his head and said that he hoped whatever they were assigned would in the future once again get them an invite to go fishing. He had never been big on fishing until the several experiences of going fishing with Alex where not only did he always catch a fish, but he got to witness the star detective demonstrate her unbelievable markswomanship.

The Chief laughed and said he agreed and said that he believed Trevor had just coined a new word.

Johnnie focused in on the defense lawyer and commented that it was clear that she was surprised by the charge of money laundering and tax evasion being brought up first.

And that the charge of attempting to kill an officer of the law would be brought up at a later time.

He put the words, "Whoa, what is happening here. I was ready to plead not guilty to attempted murder. I know my client is guilty as sin of money laundering and not paying his taxes," into the defense lawyer's mouth.

That brought a chuckle from everyone in the room.

The judge then ruled that the case would move to the next stage. He stated that the requested bail was denied and because he thought that Adriano posed a flight risk his passport was to be seized.

The judge also said that he was having Adriano sent to a Federal Bureau of Prisons detention facility where he would be held throughout his trial and then after his trial if found guilty, he might be sent to some other facility. He added that his waiting time in prison would count as time served.

The entire proceeding took less than a half hour.

Adriano walked out in a state of shocked at the speed at which the proceeding had taken place and he was dismayed when he realized that he would be taken back to a prison where he would reside throughout his trial. It did not matter that his time would count to any sentence that might be imposed.

He had come to realize that time in a cell and the brief time out in a fenced in outdoor area made him feel like he was a chicken in a hen house. It was not a roam free environment and the thought that most chicken as they aged were made into chicken soup.

Nothing had gone the way he had expected it to go.

Once again, he experienced the strange feeling that he had engaged a person who had strange powers. Powers that he had never faced before in his lifetime. He looked around expecting to see that person and shook his head as he was told to change into the orange jump suit.

She had become a shadow fighter that had handedly defeated him. A shadow fighter that he would dwell on wondering how she had pulled it all off. A shadow fighter that had anticipated his every move.

Alex meanwhile asked the Chief where he wanted to have lunch.

The Chief pointed to Johnnie and said that he would go to any place recommended by the departments food expert.

Trevor commented that he wanted a river scene so he could once again observe Johnnie watching logs floating down the Ohio.

Johnnie smiled and named a newly opened restaurant that claimed a great view of the river and the best food in the city. He added that good food always accompanied a good view of the river.

Alex commented that she expected him to pay since he would soon be getting a rich reward from the IRS for having turned in the information that was the basis for their case.

The Chief said he would have to look into who would get the money since Johnnie was on his payroll.

Alex nodded and made the comment that the Chief could certainly challenge that but highlighted the fact that he was walking on egg shells since Johnnie's action might be considered illegal.

The Chief replied that he would focus on lunch and that he knew of no illegal actions being taken by any of his detectives or their supports.

Alex laughed and suggested that they get to lunch so they could all watch Johnnie watching logs float down river.

After arriving, getting their drinks, and putting in their orders. They discussed the court proceedings until the food arrived at the table. They were all sitting at a table that had a great view of the River.

Johnnie had order a T-bone steak and a baked potato. When the food had all been placed in front of him, he did look out on the river. He suddenly stood up and pointed and said that he saw a body entangled in the limbs of the tree floating by.

Trevor was about to make a smart remark about it when he stood, pointed, and said that he saw the body too.

The Chief made a call and before the log went out of view, they saw a police boat speeding toward it.

Alex looked at the team and suggested they focus on enjoying their meal because Johnnie had most likely just identified their next assignment.

Johnnie said that he was going to enjoy his steak and not look at the river for the rest of the time they were at lunch.

Little did anyone at the table know how right Alex was in her prediction. It would take the Cincinnati team up the river to crimes committed for several generations that had been occurring from Steubenville down the Ohio river to Marietta. These crimes were illegal but very profitable and had been happening for at least one hundred years.

The End

Preview of: Moonshine

1 The Hooch and the Fortune

Hillary, her feet hanging over the edge of the cliff watched the black waters of the river below as the sky slowly changed to a mix of orange, yellow and pink. The sun seemed determined to drive the dark of the early morning back to where night hid from the day. The striking red color of the ferns along the cliff to her left and the layers of greyish blue along the mountain ridges out to the far horizon mesmerized her. She was taking a break from her morning hike that she had added to her regular visits to the stills that she owned and had hired still operators to operate.

She had spent the last few years acquiring and partnering with still operators across most of the state.

She enjoyed many an early morning hike as she was doing at the moment. Just as often it was an evening trip where she watched the sunset. It was a business that she had never dreamt that she would be running. She now considered herself the "Hooch Shine Mama."

She credited her grandmother and her own partying life to having gotten her into her current business.

Her grandmother had always talked about her "Appalachian culture." The culture was actually rooted in their Scottish roots, which went back to the sixteen hundreds Scotland. She was fascinated by her family history. It was one rooted in maintain their personal independence.

She was in her final year at junior college when her grandmother died and left her two million dollars. She was surprised by the amount and that her grandmother who had live a long life had been able to accumulate so much money.

The money represented a branch in the road that took her life in an entirely new direction. The inheritance made her question what she wanted to do. She had applied to several colleges but knew she had no real desire to pursue that path. She was an outdoor mountain girl.

The question of what she wanted to do drove her to the edge of sanity. She needed to find something other than working in an office.

Then one night at a friend's party she was introduced to a young man, Crayton Taylor. It was not a romantic attraction. She was mesmerized when he got a little drunk and told her about what he did to make a living.

He handed her an open quart jar filled with a clear liquid that had a faint tangy, pungent, malty, smell with a hint of alfalfa. She wondered whether it was tequila. Before tasting it, she asked what it was.

He proudly said that it was the hooch that was the icing on the money he made. He pushed the bottle toward her mouth and told her to take a sip.

She took a small sip and realized that he was talking about moonshine.

The smooth way it warmed her throat as it went down, followed by the warming of her stomach made her want another sip. She took another small sip and complemented him on how good it tasted and how smooth it was.

He smiled and said that it was a family recipe that each generation had worked on improving. He claimed he was the fourth generation of moonshiners and that his hooch had taken the taste up a notch.

He took another sip and handed the jar back to her.

She remembered laughing and joking as they passed the moonshine back and forth.

The next morning, he woke up in her bed and asked her how he had gotten there.

She smiled, told him that the two of them had finished the quart of his moonshine and she that she had barely been able to help him to her apartment. She asked him if he wanted to go out for breakfast.

He said that he would love to, but he needed to go up the mountain and get his still into action and then he needed to get to his day job.

She asked if after breakfast she could go along and be of help.

He nodded and said that if she could stay at the still, she could make sure that the temperature on the still did not go too high. He suggested that she bring a cooler with lunch and some drinks.

He drove his pickup to a where a small single lane road left the highway. He drove for about a mile and parked well into the brush. He then walked over to a narrow path that made its way through the brush. The trail looked more like a deer trail than a hiking trail. He carried her red metal cased cooler as if it were a feather and led the way up.

She was challenged by the slope up the mountain as she followed behind his almost jogging pace. He kept looking behind to make sure she was keeping up. He explained that he was late and needed to make it back to work in about forty-five minutes.

They were probably half way up to the top of the mountainside when he turned off the trail and led the way through a thick stand of trees.

Suddenly ahead of them was a rather large depression surrounded by rock and in the middle was a forest green elongated building that was about a highway lane wide. As they got closer, she could see through its horizontal boards and see three bright polished copper tanks.

She breathed in and seemed to both smell and taste the sweet, spicy, and fruity aroma as she walked in the door.

He led her in and proudly pointed to the three polished round copper structures that to her looked like large thermos bottles. The middle thermos was the largest.

The first one was next in size and the final thermos, whose output went to a fifty-gallon drum, was the smallest.

He explained that the still was a fifty-gallon, ten foot high still and that the thump keg and worm box made the entire structure fourteen feet long.

He pointed to a pipe that was bringing in water to cool the distillate at the last stage. He said that the water from the spring at the outer edge of the depression was one of the secrets of the great taste of the hooch.

He handed her a small glass and asked her to taste it.

She was surprised that it had a unique flavor that most waters lacked. She wondered what chemical was dissolved in it.

He said that this was the day that he was kicking off the actual distillations cycle that would extend out for about three weeks and during that time would, if everything were kept in control, produce fifty gallons of pure hooch.

He looked at her and asked whether she could stay and monitor the temperatures and make sure the gas burner stayed on and that the cooling water pump would stay on.

Hillary had nothing planned and said she would.

He pointed to the cot that was against one wall and said that she could take a nap if she needed one.

He added that there was a great view of the valley when the trail reached the top of the ridge, and she might enjoy the hike there.

He smiled and added that the black berries along the way were all getting ripe and might make the hike even more enjoyable. He told her to also look for the few gooseberry bushes along the way. They were golden in color and pure joy in taste.

He said he had to go and disappeared.

She watched the still operate for about an hour and realized that it seemed to be doing whatever it was supposed to. Everything was stable and there was nothing for her to do.

She decided that the hike up the trail was a good idea. She was constantly stopping to pick blackberries. The dark blackberries had a tart bordering on sweet and tangy flavor, while unripe berries were on the sour or bitter side. She only found one bush of goose berries, but they were truly pure joy to taste.

She got to the top and sat down on a boulder set a few feet back from the edge of a cliff that ended below in the jumble of jagged pieces of what had once been the face of the cliff.

She decided to call Crayton and ask a few questions about running the still.

She asked the cost of the materials that he put into the still.

He said that he normally spent about five hundred dollars for the grain that he put in.

She asked how much he sold a quart for.

He responded that for a quart he was currently getting fifteen dollars.

She did the math in her head and figured that each batch was worth three thousand dollars, so the margin was twenty-five hundred dollars.

That would be thirty-six thousand dollars a year.

She asked him how long the production season ran.

He let her know that he had extended it from the beginning of May to the end of October and he managed to get seven batches done during that time.

He added that he was working on shortening the time to make each batch to two weeks by preparing the mash ferment in a separate container. He said that approach would double his production.

She shook her head when she realized that he was currently making only eighteen thousand dollars for his efforts, and he was risking getting arrested, facing up to five years in prison and being fined ten thousand dollars.

She went back to the still and found a pencil and paper and spent the rest of the day figuring out how many stills were needed to make the risk an attractive choice.

The page she had scribbled on was totally covered when she decided that she would needed to control sixty stills to make it a worthwhile venture. When she factored in his doubling of his current production it dropped down to a more reasonable thirty stills. That was still a big number.

She wondered whether there were that many stills in existence and if not if there were that many locations available to put them.

She looked at the still in front of her and realized that there was enough space in the current building to put in two more stills.

That would reduce the locations from thirty down to ten or fifteen separate locations.

She could envision operating that many.

She then wondered how difficult it would be to get the amount of materials for three stills up and put in place. She also wondered if she could find the operators for all the stills.

She figured her best bet was to recruit existing moonshiners and see what kind of deal she could arrange with them. If the sites used by the moonshiners was big enough, she could triple their operations.

She figured they would be making three times as more money would attract most of them.

She knew that she was taking a branch in the road that she had never dreamt of. It was a branch that had a high risk, but it also had a high reward. It was certainly not a traditional line of work. She laughed and thought that she would label it as a career in mountain side hiking, hooch making and fun.

Not much later she proposed expanding Crayton's operation. He said he liked the idea. He would be able to quit his current line cooking job and spend his entire time running three stills.

He asked how they would split the money they made. She suggested that for the first year after the additional two stills were on line, he get one hundred percent of what they sold. Then his take would drop to seventy percent.

She pointed out that it would be almost twice as much as his current income counting his day job and running his one still.

He said that sounded like a great deal for him but what about her?

Hillary said that she hoped that he would help her make similar deals with enough other moonshiners so that she could get enough from each still that she would make a small fortune.

He nodded and said that he knew of about six other people running stills, but he figured he could ask around and get more names. He was not sure if they would all be interested but he figured if she expanded their businesses, they would likely take her up on a similar deal to his.

It took her only three years to expand her moonshine business to the point that she was partners with eighteen operators that in total operated fifty-one stills.

She was shy of the sixty stills that she had at one time estimated she would need when she had done her first calculations, but it put her close enough that she figured that it was time for her to recoup her investment before going any farther.

She smiled as she looked in the mirror, realized that she had taken that other branch in the road and that she was happy about her choice.

<u>*2 Dam Right*</u>

Samuel stood on the grated metal walkway of the dam looking into the clear water that seemed to go down to a deep black depth. He could see fish eating the gear algae growing off the walls of the dam. The water of the Ohio was still clear, but Samuel knew that even this high up the river, the pollution whether visible of not was already in the river.

The Pittsburg buildings and factories were spewing their waste all along its banks.

As a dam lock gate operator, he also saw how the tugs seemed to treat the river as their garbage disposal container. He often envisioned not opening up the lock for one of the polluting tugs and making them pay a fine. It was a fantasy that he knew would never happen.

He had grown up boating, swimming in and fishing in the Ohio. His family owned a cottage on its bank and had a pier that ran a short distance out. This was where during the warm weather months they kept their ski boat and the fishing boat that was his father's pride and joy.

He still went out almost every weekend fishing with his dad.

Skiing was still high on his list, but his dad had more or less turned the black twenty-five-foot ski boat with its two one hundred horsepower outboard engines over to him.

It was usually he and his friends that did the skiing almost every weekend of the summer. He usually held a grill out on the pier.

They would ski off the end of the pier. He was a good enough skier that he could take off from the pier, ski up the river and on the return, he would let go close enough that he would ski in toward the side ladder and get on it before the water got above his knees.

It was his way of showing off to the young women that were watching.

He knew that he was fortunate to be living the good life.

His job as a lock operator was rather boring except when a barge was coming through the lock. At this stage in the river, most tugs were only pushing a couple of barges. His lock could only handle three at a time. This meant any ambitious tug operators choosing to push more than three barges needed to make more than one trip through the lock. The process of going through was time-consuming and most operators chose not to do so.

He and his friends often spent Friday nights at Mallard's Bar and Dance Club in downtown Weirton. The normal routine was to meet for dinner, sit and drink beer, and then dance the night away.

He lived within walking distance which allowed him leeway in how much he drank.

It was during one of these nights where a friend of his introduced him to Hillary. He enjoyed the evening chatting and dancing with her.

He was disappointed when she turned him down when he invited her to his apartment but perked up when she said she would love watching a barge go through the lock.

It was during her visit to watch a barge go through that she invited him to come down and party with her in Wheeling.

He accepted and the weekend he went to Wheeling and enjoying a great night dancing she invited him to her apartment.

Since then, he had been in Wheeling about once a month.

So far, he could not figure out how she made her living, but he learned that she traveled throughout West Virginia checking on her business investments. He was really curious what type of investments one could make in the state that would have you traveling around to check on it. He figured it had to be property and that she was some sort of realtor.

He wanted to go to the next level with her, but it was clear that she was not ready for anything like that, so he focused on his job and periodically going to Wheeling.

He knew that he was living the good life and that she seemed to be the last piece to that puzzle, but she seemed to be just out of his reach.

Hillary indeed was not ready. She liked Sam and enjoyed spending time with him, but she had similar relationships with at least a half dozen other very handsome and virile young men.

Sam was the oldest of those and the one that seemed the most stable and held the most promise, but she knew that she wanted to do much more before she settled down and settling down was at the bottom of the list.

She pushed forward and focused intensely on the expansion of her business.

She found that it took time to befriend the still operators. Many seemed to be from the shy and recluse side of the social spectrum. In each case she spent time to get to know them where they operated their still. She partied with each of them and learned who their friends were.

Several of her prospects were true loners and she spent significant time just getting to the point where they would sit with her at the bar and share a drink with her. She was often more successful asking if they would take her hunting.

When she was introduced to them at a bar, getting to their stills was often even more of a challenge.

The challenge multiplied when she got into proposing the expansion of their moonshine business. She lost that challenge to two of them but the rest, once they understood her proposal, accepted. Later when they realized how much more money, they were making they thanked her for being patient with them.

Some of the still operators ended up in her apartment but most did not. She had straight business relationship with most of them.

She spent more than two years and most of her inheritance expanding her still kingdom and making each still almost three times as productive as they had previously been.

She had to drastically sharpen her marketing and distribution capability in order to move the increased moonshine volume that each still was producing. She moved more volume by decreasing the unit cost of each jar of moonshine, and she was smart enough to decrease the quantity in each jar by a few ounces.

She also had to get the people running her stills to be more productive.

She coached them on how to time their three stills so that the work was balanced.

She made a point setting up a schedule of bringing up the materials for the still so that the work was distributed throughout the week or month.

The same was true for bottling and then distributing the moonshine.

She made sure that she watched the futures market to get the best price on corn and the other ingredients and set up a central distribution hub where all her still operators picked up their supplies.

Her ability to organize her supply chain, the production and distribution system was an example of supply chain management that would have ranked among the best in the country but of course she could not share what she was doing. Had Ford been alive and known what she was doing he would have been proud of her and named her his star pupil.

She did all this on a minimum of sleep and a minimum of partying.

It took its toll.

One morning as she brushed her hair and looked in the mirror, she saw a white streak of hair on the left side of her head. She held that strand of white out and looked at it for at least ten minutes. Then she laughed because she realized that her business was finally producing the cash flow that she had calculated that day, just a few years past, when she had figured what it would take for her to build her moonshine empire.

It had cost her but now she was in control of a business that was churning out the cash that was rushing into her money well. It was as if it was being pumped in by a powerful water pump. In the next year she would recoup her more than two million dollars of investment and then in the following year she would more than triple the money that she had started out with.

Life could return back closer to normal. She could take time to enjoy some parties with her friends.

Layton had been one of the still operators who had taken the deal to expand his moonshine making operation. The increase in his income meant he could quit being a common laborer and enjoy some of the other pleasures such as chasing some skirts and partying on the weekends.

As his still operation tripled in volume, he realized that he was working harder than when he ran only one still and worked as a general laborer. After a year he came to the conclusion that what he was making was not enough and that he was going to demand a bigger share than he was currently getting. He figured he was in a great position to do so.

Hillary was surprised when Layton, the operator that she recognized as the least capable, producing the least and least trustworthy demanded a bigger share of the take. She knew that was not going to happen.

She explained to him that he was getting the biggest portion of the money that his three stills were producing and that he had the same deal she had with every other still operator. She shared that every one of those operators had let her know that they felt it was a great deal and were very happy about it.

Layton listened and negatively shook his head and said he didn't believe what she was telling him. He figured she was getting most of the money being raked in on the moonshine he was operating.

Hillary took him through the books that she kept on his still operation. She explained the arrangement, drew it out on paper so she could show how the finances were managed and the fact that his still was actually making slightly less than most of the others.

Layton got angry and accused her of trying to confuse him and that he was going to bring in the DEA and share what he knew about her operation if he didn't get a better percentage.

Hillary decided that she needed to meet his demand, until she could figure a way to get rid of him.

It was as if he had read her mind, he pulled out a pistol, that she recognized as a thirty-eight or something similar, and threatened to shoot her if she didn't double what she was currently paying him.

She recognized the danger she was in, nodded and said that she would write him a check for the money.

He said he did not want a check but wanted cash and that the two of them should go to the bank and get it.

She put her check book away and said that they should go down to her car and go to the bank. On the way down the path, she waited until the trail took a sharp turn and then grabbed his gun hand and turned it upward and under his chin.

Layton was surprised by the move and inadvertently pulled the trigger and killed himself.

Hillary was shocked by what had happened. She looked around to make sure no one was on the trail or in the woods. She pulled Layton's body back into the brush. She was thinking hard about what she needed to do.

She needed to get rid of the body and she needed to get someone to run the still.

Two people came to mind.

Crayton, her first and best still operator, had his stills only fifty miles away. She would offer him the opportunity to more than double his income if he ran both operations. She figured he would be willing since it would put him into a much better financial position. He was one of the still operators that she had come to trust.

Getting rid of the body was a little more of a sensitive issue. She thought about burying him somewhere on the mountain side but figured it might be too easily discovered by hunters or dug up by animals.

She decided to call Samuel to see if he might help her figure out what to do.

Samuel listened to Hillary explain what had happened. He said that he knew how to handle the situation and that they should do it that night.

He told her to meet him at the bottom of the trail. He would bring his pickup to where the trail came out of the forest. He would go up with her and bring the body in the back and then take the body to the Ohio river, weigh it down and dump it down stream of the dam where he worked. He figured the body would sink to the bottom and decay. It would never be discovered.

Hillary thanked him. She led him to Layton's body, followed his pickup to the dam, and watched as the body totally wrapped with a heavy-duty link chain was dumped into the river. She noted that Samuel threw the gun into the river as well.

She then followed Samuel to his favorite bar where they spent the evening dancing and having a few brews.

That night was the first time she went to his apartment.

It was also the first night of a long rain storm that set a new record for rainfall in a single week. By the middle of that drenching the Ohio river level rose to the point that for the first time since he had been hired, he had to open the gates to the dam's flood overflow passage.

The flow of the water was so high that trees and a ton of debris washed down river.

Hillary had gone to the river and stood almost a block back from the banks of the river and wondered where Layton's body might end up.

Thank you for reading the far.

Go to the website below to get the book.

About the Author

Ronald E. Mueller

remwriter95@gmail.com

Ron grew up in what is now Flint River State Park in Southeast Iowa. The 170-year-old house Ron lived in is built into a hillside. It faces a 125-foot-high cliff towering over the little Flint River. The house and the land talked to him about; the passing of time, the struggle to conquer the land, the struggles people faced and the wonder of nature.

He climbed the cliffs, crawled into the caves, dove from the swimming rock, collected clams from the bottom of the pond, gigged and skinned frogs for their legs. He trapped muskrats for fur, hunted raccoon in the dead of night, and with only a stick hunted rabbits in the dead of winter.

His young life was outdoors, and nature tested him.

He walked to a one room stone schoolhouse uphill both ways. A stern but warm-hearted teacher, Mrs. Henry was instrumental in shaping his character as she shepherded him from the fourth to the eighth grade. A Montessori before its time. It was a great way to grow up.

Ron graduated from Burlington, High School, went to Vietnam in the Navy. He graduated from The University of South Florida with an master's degree in engineering, worked for thirty eight years for Procter and Gamble, traveled around the world thirty times.

He has remained happily married for more than fifty years. His daughter and his two sons are all successful and his three grandchildren have all graduated.

His wife has humored and supported him as he became a full time professional story teller.

His experiences inter-twined with snippets of fantasy lend themselves to the adventures he leads the reader through.

Books by the Author

Fiction Series
The Alex Evercrest Series
The River Front
The Girl on The Grill
Missing
Maggot
Racist
Votive Candles
Windy City
Country Road
Pool of Blood
Sins of the Daughter
Body Parts
The Skull Collector
The Vanishing
The Shadow Fighter
Moonshine
Grief's Trajectory
The Magic Touch
Northern Lights
Alex Evercrest Heroine
Alex Evercrest Collection Two
New Direction
A Family Affair
Disruption
The St. Lebuinnus Church Murder

A Brian O'Neil Novel
Hawaiian Phoenix
Moon Curser
Death Broker

The Problem Solver Series
Solutions
Drug Lords
Border Crosser
The Problem Solver Collection

The Taelo Series
Taelo: The Early Years
Taelo: The Golden Feather
Taelo: Journey of Discovery
Taelo: Dangerous Passage
Taelo: Condor Clan Slingers
Taelo: Circumvention
Taelo: The Journey of Sages
Taelo: Collection
Taelo: Future Leaders Journey

A Taelo Story:
White Swan and Quiet Pheasant
The Child's Name
Floating Cloud
Quiet Rabbit
Busy Bee
Little Otter & Talking Wren
Broken Spear

Burley Bear & Meadow Flower
Taelo Story Collection
<u>Science Fiction</u>
The Savitar Series
Journey's End
Savitar
Confluence
Savitar Series Collection

The Door Series
The Door
Aliens We
The Endless Hole
The Swarm
Esoteric Journey
The Gentle Eye
The Door Series Collection

Bram Nielson Series
The Fold
The Message
Fold Wormhole
Negative Fold
Ripples in Time
Bram Nielson Collection

<u>Single Science Fiction Books</u>
Current Past and Future
The Event
The Door
Viajante 7

Characters in the Story

Alex	Cathy	Evercrest	Police Detective
Matthew	Timothy	Knolton	Alex's suitor
Rose-Anne	Germain	Evercrest	Alex's mother
Russel	Johnson	Evercrest	Alex father
Helping Hands charity			Alex's nonprofit org
Trey		McGregor	Alex Detective Partner
Lindsey		McGregor	Wife
Nolan		McGregor	Son
Johnnie		Smith	Old Viet Vet
Mary		Higgins	Johnnie's Phili "friend"
Bruce	Lincoln	Johnson	Cinci Chief of Detect
Mary-Anne	Leslie	Johnson	Chiefs Wife
Bill	Hamilton	Danson	Detective
Travis	Bailey	Carter	Detective
Dr. Rogers			Coroner
Jane	Elousie	Stradford	Lieutenant Governor
Felix			proprietor fishing dock
Golden Goose			Name of the Yacht
Sandra		Olson	Policewoman guard
Annie	Lorie	Scots	Missing girl
Linda		Annies	older daughter
Lorie		Annies	second daughter
Harold		Zimmerman	Chicago DEA
James	Oscor	Kaizer	Sheriff of Wiggin
Abbie	Alisa	Bender	protect Alex married James
John	S.	Williams	Lawyer that was abused
Hanna		Waverly	John's mate
Angelica			Angel on the hill
Brian		Lexter	Cinci FBI Bureau Chief
Cais		Leu	Alex's Viet friend
Tracy		Hunter	Trey's Analyst
Adriano			Chicago Mafia Boss
Lorenzo			Italian Sniper
Ray			Mafia gunmen
Baily			Mafia gunmen
Andy		Weller	IRS lawyer - Chicago
Lenord		Maxwell	Chicago lawyer

www.remwriter95.net/

Published by: Around the World Publishing LLC.